"If You Think You Can Charm Your Way Into My Life Again, You're Even Cockier Than I Thought.

"I'm surprised you'd let your hormones override the biggest business deal either of our firms have ever seen."

In his slow, easy manner, Cole moved across the room. "You're right. But, I just had to know."

"Know what?"

"If the sparks were still there." Cole stood squarely before her, leaned to her ear and whispered, "They are."

Dear Reader,

Falling in love for the first time is not only exciting; it can be a bit scary venturing into unknown territory. I have to say, I've never been on a more rewarding adventure than to have married my first love.

I cannot think of a better way to express my love and celebrate my eleventh wedding anniversary this past September to my high school sweetheart than the release of *From Boardroom to Wedding Bed?*

In this reunion story, you will soon discover that like most people, Cole and Tamera never forgot the first time they fell in love. Now fate, and a career in the same field, has given them a second chance at a love so rare, so perfect.

I hope you experience all the emotions with Cole and Tamera as you did the first time you fell head over stilettos. :)

Much love,

Jules

JULES BENNETT

FROM BOARDROOM TO WEDDING BED?

Published by Silhouette Books
America's Publisher of Contemporary Romance

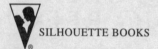 **SILHOUETTE BOOKS**

ISBN-13: 978-0-373-73059-9

Recycling programs for this product may not exist in your area.

FROM BOARDROOM TO WEDDING BED?

Copyright © 2010 by Jules Bennett

Printed in U.S.A.

Books by Jules Bennett

Silhouette Desire

Seducing the Enemy's Daughter #2004
For Business...or Marriage? #2010
From Boardroom to Wedding Bed? #2046

JULES BENNETT

Jules's love of storytelling started when she would get in trouble as a child and would tell her parents her imaginary friend Mimi did it. Since then her vivid imagination has taken her down a path she'd only dreamed of.

When Jules isn't spending time with her wonderful supportive husband and two daughters, you will find her reading her favorite authors, though she calls that time "research." She loves to hear from readers! Contact her at julesbennett@falcon1.net, visit her Web site at www.julesbennett.com or send her a letter at P.O. Box 396, Minford, OH 45653.

For my first, my only, my love…Michael. *Ti Amo*

One

"I'm offering the contract to...both of you."

Panic surged through Tamera Stevens as she jerked upright in her plush, leather seat at the same time Cole Marcum exclaimed, "You're serious?"

"I settle for nothing less than the best." Victor Lawson, world-renowned hotelier, spread his hands wide and tilted back in his leather chair. "Having my first hotel in the U.S. designed by the top architects in the country is what I want. If this is a problem, I need to know before anything is signed. I hope we can all work together to make this the biggest, grandest hotel not only to come to Miami, but to the entire country."

Problem? Oh, no. No problem at all, Tamera thought as she fought the urge to cry, scream or just race from the boardroom. Could they hear the rapid thump, thump, thump of her heart beating against her chest? Had perspiration already broken out along her top lip or forehead? God, if she didn't breathe she was going to pass out.

So, aside from the fact that Cole Marcum, her once fiancé, had broken her heart back in college and this was the first time she'd seen him in over a decade, no, there was no problem.

Oh, and now they were going to be forced to work together because no one, absolutely no one would turn down the chance to work with Victor Lawson.

Dandy, just dandy. Yup, this would be a problem-free work zone.

She wanted to throw up on her trendy silver pumps. If she and Cole agreed to this once-in-a-lifetime opportunity, they would be spending every waking moment together for months.

A lifetime had passed since they'd spent every waking, and several sleeping, moments together. Being together in such a tight-knit environment would certainly test her strength in taking over The Stevens Group and proving she was just as powerful and capable as her father of running the family's multimillion-dollar company.

But, did she really have to spend so much time with Cole? Couldn't she work with someone else in his firm? She was having a hard enough time being in this meeting that had only lasted ten minutes.

"I've never worked with another agency on a design," Cole spoke up, causing every nerve ending in Tamera's body to shiver. "A Marcum design is priceless and unique."

So, he still had a high opinion of himself? Obviously his ego had grown through the years since his abrupt departure.

Tamera couldn't deny the fact Cole had gotten even sexier as he'd aged, but his curl-your-toes, exotic good looks were merely a facade covering up the ugly persona beneath a billion-dollar smile and expensive, Italian suits.

She wished she could go into this amazing, once-in-a-lifetime opportunity with the excitement that came along with new projects, but how could she when the devil himself sat next to her?

Victor nodded, leaning forward to rest his elbows on the gleaming mahogany table. The billionaire was only in his late thirties, but he'd done more in his young years with his European businesses than many people do in a lifetime. With his blond hair, tanned skin, and blue eyes, he looked like the all-American playboy. And from the rumors and tabloids, he was known worldwide for breaking women's hearts.

"I understand your concern and confusion, Mr. Marcum, but I assure you, both of you, that this will be beneficial for all of us."

Beneficial? Business-wise, sure. On a personal level, this could be detrimental to her health and her heart. She'd had to put it back together piece by shattered piece. Was fate offering up the ultimate test to see how she would measure up?

Dammit. Why did he have to look even better than what she'd remembered? Those broad shoulders beneath his charcoal suit, coal black hair and chiseled facial features were only more of a distraction.

Yes, he looked every bit the professional, but he also looked a bit rugged with those hard, dark-as-night eyes that held you in your place.

Did he smile anymore? Was his demeanor just as cool as his stare? As a businessman, Cole and his twin brother Zach were sharks, but on a personal level, what was Cole like now?

No. She would not be swept into his world again. She would not sit and wonder what he did in his spare time. She would not think about the women who'd come through his life since he'd left her hurt and confused. She was a professional and she would remain as one, especially during the duration of this development.

Cole was extremely sexy, but sexy men were everywhere, especially in Miami. This man was no big deal. Really. Just because he'd taken her virginity, offered her the world and promised to love her forever, she wasn't about to sit around and pine over a dream that died long ago.

She was stronger now and had much more pressing matters to worry about than being slapped in the face with her past.

Like the fact that her father was nearing the end of his life.

Which was just one more reason why she had to get this project. Now that the CEO position had been turned over to her, she couldn't disappoint anyone in the company, especially her father. She wanted to prove to him, before he passed, that she would take care of the company that had been in their family for three generations.

Other than the caregivers she'd hired, no one knew of his illness. No one could. Stocks would fall and clients would pull projects if word spread about her father's sudden diagnosis with stage four lung cancer.

Walter Stevens *was* The Stevens Group. He'd worked at that firm before he went to college. He'd started at the lowest level and worked his way up and there wasn't a contractor in the business who didn't know him on a first-name basis. Which meant she had to be on her game with Victor Lawson. Errors, even of the smallest proportions, were unacceptable.

And Cole could never find out why her father was not in charge. He would use the untimely hardship to his advantage and she refused to allow him the upper hand in her life ever again. Or any man for that matter.

She supposed she should thank Cole. Because of his heartless act, she was stronger, more independent.

"I want this to be extravagant," Victor went on to say. "I want Miami and the entire world to see the passion behind this structure, the sexiness behind the elegance. People come to Miami to get away. I want them to be swept away to another time. I want lovers to feel like they are fulfilling a fantasy."

With any other project, the word "lover" wouldn't set her nerve endings on edge. This wasn't like any other project, though.

Tamera summoned all her will to fight and all of the B.S. she could handle to the surface. "Mr. Lawson, I can't speak for my associate, but I can speak on behalf of The Stevens Group when I say we would be delighted to work on this design with any firm of your choosing. We are anxious to get started."

Take that, Cole, Mr. I'm-Calling-Off-the-Engagement-and-I-Don't-Need-to-Provide-a-Reason.

Great, now she was turning juvenile. Poking jabs at her colleagues this early in the game would only cause problems…something she definitely didn't need right now. Especially with Victor's talk of "passion" and "sexiness."

Victor offered a triumphant smile and she nearly applauded her performance.

"I'm happy to hear that. I expected no less. Even though your father has started his retirement on such short notice, I knew any child of his would come through for me."

"Mr. Marcum?" Victor turned his attention to Cole. "You have nothing to lose here. You will not be splitting the money. You will each get the agreed amount when you put in your bids. That is only fair. Keep in mind I've never done that before, but I budgeted in the extra amount and with the design you two come up with, I'm sure I will still turn a nice profit from my investment in your companies."

His high hopes in her abilities only made the quivering in her stomach that much more erratic. And, she couldn't correct Victor's assumption of her father's "retirement." To anyone other than herself and the doctors and nurses, her father *was* in retirement. If only that could be the simple truth.

She'd been in her father's company since graduating college, working from the ground up just like he had. And now she was the CEO, though she would give the prestigious position up in a heartbeat if that meant her father could be well and come back to work.

Tamera inwardly sighed and steeled herself against the bubbling of past feelings as she, too, turned her attention to wait for Cole's answer. Past or no past, Tamera found herself intrigued by his powerful, sexy presence. If she were meeting him for the first time, she'd be interested in seeing him on a personal level. And that was saying quite a bit considering she hadn't found herself wanting to ask any man out lately. Not in years, in fact.

Where had the time gone? Obviously by the wayside with her nonexistent sex life.

Had she really turned into that thirtysomething

woman who had given up on happiness and relationships all because of one bad experience?

"If this is the only way we can work a deal, then I'm in, too."

Tamera breathed a sigh of relief, yet cringed at the thought of working with Cole. Yes, she wanted this job more than anything, but she really thought he'd put up more of a fight about working with her.

Could they actually pretend there was nothing between them? Their past was the proverbial elephant in the room and the darn thing had plopped down right between them, though Cole's cold stare and demeanor left her feeling foolish. Seems he wasn't as affected by her presence as she was by his.

Had Victor picked up on the tension or was he too caught up in his latest venture?

Working with Cole would be fine, she assured herself. Seriously, what choice did she really have here?

Professional. She would remain professional no matter what and the past would just have to stay where she'd left it eleven years ago…along with her heart.

"Excellent." Victor came to his feet. Tamera and Cole followed. "I'll have the contracts drawn up and sent to your offices. I hope to have them to you by the end of the week so we can get started. I will also send over a more detailed list of all my requirements and some of my own ideas. Questions or concerns should be addressed directly to me. Also, please feel free to step outside the box, literally. Get out of your offices and work where your creativity can flow without the interruptions of faxes, phones or assistants. Let yourself get carried away with this fantasy as you design."

Get carried away with the fantasy? No thanks. Been there, done that, got the broken heart as a souvenir.

Tamera shook Victor's hand, grabbed her designer handbag and headed out the door. Meeting over, no need to stick around and torture herself one more second than necessary with the crisp scent of Cole's cologne. Though she may as well get used to the agony. Working on this project would take months and she had a feeling this was just a small portion of what was in store for her.

Tamping down on the hurt of past memories, Tamera took the glass elevator down to the lobby of Victor Lawson's newest office building.

She was a professional now, not the twenty-two-year-old-girl who was young and in love with the man who'd promised her the world and then left her for no good reason. Oh, he'd mumbled something about being too young and getting engaged too fast, but she didn't believe that. Something happened to make him change his mind.

Whatever it was, if he wasn't strong enough to fight for her and what they had, she didn't want him. She was just surprised that someone like Cole, who'd seemed so in charge of his life and had a good grasp of where he was going, would take the easy way out when it came to love.

And if Cole Marcum was expecting her to be that same innocent girl, he would be sorely disappointed. She didn't have time to stroll down the broken path that led to memory lane. She had a company to run and a father to care for.

No, she didn't have time to even give Cole a second thought.

So why, from the moment the meeting started, was he the only topic in the forefront of her mind?

"Get in my office."

Cole slid his iPhone back into his pocket and paced

in what he liked to call the "pace space"—the area between his oversized chrome and glass desk and the large windows overlooking Miami's harbor and the countless yachts lining the dock.

Tamera Stevens.

Could the tightness in his chest be more bothersome? Hadn't enough years gone by to erase that band of guilt squeezing his heart? How could he have time to feel guilty for hurting Tamera, though, when he was running a multimillion-dollar company? Yes, he'd moved on and hadn't looked back. That didn't mean he was happy with the way he'd treated someone he'd deeply cared for.

But Victor Lawson merely piled on more guilt when he dropped the bomb that the two architectural firms would be working together. And not just the firms, but he'd specifically asked for Tamera and Cole to design the resort themselves. No assistants needed. No structural engineers to step in. Just the heads of the companies.

Fate was a fickle woman.

"What's up?"

Cole didn't stop pacing even when his twin, Zach, came to stand on the other side of the desk.

"We got the Lawson project," Cole told him as he stopped to look at the harbor, wishing he could be out on his own yacht.

"And your chipper tone is due to the fact that you hate signing multimillion-dollar deals with the biggest business mogul in the world?"

Cole threw a glance over his shoulder. "Sarcasm is not appreciated right now. We have to work with another firm on this."

That got Zach's attention. "Who?"

Turning back to the beauty of the water, Cole clenched his teeth. "The Stevens Group."

"Walter Stevens? You hate that bastard."

Wasn't that an understatement? Who wouldn't hate the man who'd threatened to ruin his future all because he fell in love with the man's daughter?

"It's a bit more complicated." Cole sighed, spun around and sat on the edge of the windowsill. "Walter isn't working on this for some reason."

"Tamera is."

Even though it wasn't a question, Cole nodded, prompting a low whistle from Zach.

"Want me to handle the design?" Zach asked. "I don't mind working with her. It actually may be best, considering."

The thought was tempting, but Cole refused to back down now. "No. I want to work with her."

"You can't be serious." Zach said. "It's been, what, eleven years? She's not going to be the same person you fell in love with, Cole. Trust me, love dies."

Cole couldn't argue the truth. And his twin knew firsthand. Zach had a marriage that didn't get much past the "I do's" before the bride took off with another man. But Cole didn't want love. He wanted Walter Stevens to see he was strong enough to be paired with his precious company and daughter. The merging of companies on this project was priceless. In fact, it was just the opportunity he'd been waiting for to show Walter Stevens he was just as powerful, if not more so, than the old man.

"What are you going to do?" Zach asked, leaning against the corner of the desk. "Are you finally going to tell her you were threatened by the old man?"

"No. She wouldn't believe me and that was so long ago, we've both moved on." So many thoughts and ideas bounced around inside his head. "Granted, I can't avoid the fact she's still the sexiest woman I've ever seen. Who knows? Maybe that sexual chemistry is still there. It would sure make for an interesting few months."

Zach let out a chuckle. "What if she's just a typical spoiled little rich girl who's stepping into shoes she can't even possibly fill?"

Cole considered the possibility. "That may be, but I don't want anything from Tamera other than a good partner on this project. Besides, she still seems sweet and innocent. Nothing like Walter."

"Sweet and innocent was probably shot straight to hell when you trampled her heart without giving her cause," Zach said, as if Cole needed the reminder. "I don't know about you, but I think a multimillion-dollar deal is far more important than lust. Will you be able to concentrate?"

The Stevens Group was one of the top design firms in the country, which made her a complete professional. They could do the job, and hopefully if that sexual attraction still existed…well…

Not that he wanted anything remotely like what they'd had. Hell no. He only wanted to see if she tasted the same, if her skin still shivered beneath his touch. What hot-blooded male wouldn't want to explore that body again?

Tamera Stevens was a typical Miami bombshell with long blonde hair, blue eyes and a body that was centerfold material. He'd be interested in her even if they'd just met. The fact that they shared a past only made the situation more intriguing.

As for love? No thanks. Any feelings remotely resembling love had died along with their dreams of a life together. Love didn't have a place in his world…not when his life consisted of nothing but his scale, butter paper and the art of design. Love was a lost emotion that Walter Stevens had personally sucked right out of him.

"I'm concentrating," Cole said with a grin. "Believe me, I'm concentrating. Tamera has no idea of the man I've become."

Zach raised a brow. "This competition isn't between you and Tamera. It's between you and her father."

Walter Stevens had never liked Cole, but when Cole proposed to Tamera the summer between their senior year of college and right before graduate school, Walter pulled out the threats.

If Cole didn't let Tam go, Walter would get Cole's scholarship taken away. Walter Stevens had connections everywhere and Cole knew the man wasn't just blowing hot air.

And because Cole, Zach and their baby sister Kayla were raised by their grandmother and basically had to scrape to get by, Cole had to give in. He had no connections and his only ticket out of near poverty was his scholarship.

Choosing between the future of his career and the future of his heart was the hardest decision he'd ever had to make…and one he'd questioned every day for a long time after the breakup. But he firmly believed everything happened for a reason and Cole was just fine with how his life had turned out.

The next few months would certainly be a challenge. But Cole was up for anything. Especially if it meant making millions—and exploring Tamera's seductive curves once again.

Two

The contracts were signed. There was no turning back.

She could do this. Working with Cole would be just like back in college at the University of Florida when they'd worked on designs together in her off-campus apartment or his dorm room.

Except now they were dealing with millions of dollars and not grades…or feelings.

Okay, so they were dealing with feelings, at least, she was. But any emotions she had were just remnants from what they had before.

What they had before? Tam rolled her eyes and shut down her computer, thankful to be going home. Anything they'd had before had been strictly one-sided or Cole wouldn't have been able to walk away without looking back. She'd gotten over the fact that he'd walked away, but what she hadn't recovered from was his reasoning…or lack thereof.

When he'd called their engagement off, Tamera was sick. She'd taken her father's advice and transferred schools so she could break ties with Cole and start new. But even though she'd moved on, she never forgot the man she'd loved with her whole heart.

The man who currently stood filling her office doorway.

"Cole." Erratic heartbeats and instant jellylike knees made her thankful she was seated behind her desk instead of standing. "What are you doing here?"

"We need to talk."

He made his way across the plush, white carpet. Even at the end of a long business day, the man still looked amazing. He'd shed his tie and jacket, leaving him in black pants and a baby blue dress shirt with the sleeves rolled up onto his tanned forearms. A bit of dark shadow around his jawline made her catch her breath.

Past or no past, this man was sexy as all get-out and she couldn't deny the fact. Why couldn't he at least have gotten an unsightly beer gut after all these years?

"I was just heading home," she told him, trying to ignore his pantherlike eyes. "If you'd like to call tomorrow, I'd be happy to discuss the initial planning of the design."

Instead of taking a seat across from her desk, like most visitors, Cole came around the side and propped a hip on the corner, mere inches from her. That same masculine cologne he'd had on during their meeting with Victor tickled and teased her senses. His broad shoulders filled his dress shirt and his lips were just as full and kissable as they were the day he'd asked her to marry him.

Mercy. Day one of…how quick could they finish this project?

"I'm not here to discuss the design."

Did the man blink? Why was he staring? Was he really that unaffected by their reunion? Surely the crackle of tension in the air wasn't only vibrating around her.

Tamera cleared her throat and scooted back a bit in her chair. She didn't pretend to misunderstand the topic he was approaching. Did he honestly believe he could barge into her office and pick up where he dropped her?

"Cole, this isn't professional. Rehashing the past won't do a thing toward getting these designs done, so why go there?"

His gaze traveled over her, making her feel even more heated than before. When his eyes roamed back to her face, he seemed to study her. Tamera hated being under a microscope.

"Are you really okay working with me?" he asked in a low, steady voice. "That's the real reason I'm here. We should discuss this arrangement without Victor or our staff present."

Damn the man for being so cool and controlled. And how dare he think she'd be withering at the thought of working with him? If the only reason he came was to make sure she was "man" enough for the job, she'd show him who would dominate this situation.

Tamera came to her feet, causing Cole to look up from his half-seated position. "This is a dream job, Cole. Brainstorming with the devil won't make me back down, so there's no need to coddle me and pretend you care about my feelings."

He smiled, but remained perched on the corner of her

desk. "Zach offered to take my place, but he's normally the on-site guy."

Even though the ache hadn't moved from her chest since she'd seen Cole a week ago at the initial meeting with Victor, she pasted on a smile and moved toward her fourth-story window and looked out onto the city lights of sultry, sexy South Beach.

"So, you two have discussed my well-being? How thoughtful. I assure you, I'll be fine. The question is, will you?"

She turned back to see his reaction and was surprised when the muscle in his jaw ticked. Cole came to his feet, closing the space between them.

Didn't the man know how to read body language? Hadn't she given him the not-so-subtle hint that she wanted space? And why did her body have to betray her by reacting to this enticing man?

"To be honest," he said, looming over her, backing her against the cool glass, "I may not be."

How did she lose control over this situation and in her own office, for crying out loud?

She moistened her lips and cursed herself when his eyes darted to her mouth. Now he chooses to read body language. Surely he wasn't going to kiss her.

"Why is that?" she asked, thankful her voice didn't crack.

"Because you're even more alluring and vivacious than you were in college. I'm intrigued."

"Good for you."

She tried to be nonchalant, but God help her, she wanted to kiss him. She wanted to feel his lips on hers again. She wasn't even going to try to lie to herself.

When they'd been together, they'd been good. For nearly two years, they'd been inseparable. Nothing and no one had come close to filling her heart the way Cole had back then. Kissing Cole would only catapult her back in time and ruin any hopes of being professional on this project.

Sanity prevailed as she shoved him back.

"No." She moved around him and went to her door, gesturing for him to leave. "If you think you can charm your way into my life again, you're even cockier than I thought. I'm surprised you'd let your hormones override the biggest business deal either of our firms has ever seen."

In his slow, easy manner, Cole moved across the room, hands shoved into his pants pockets. "You're right. But, I just had to know."

She hated to be predictable and ask, but she had to. "Know what?"

"If the sparks were still there." Cole stood squarely before her, leaned to her ear and whispered. "They are."

Without another word, he walked from her office. Whistling.

Tamera resisted the urge to slam the door. Could he be more maddening?

Whistling? Ugh! If he thought for one minute he could play around with her emotions, business, personal or otherwise, she'd show him. Nothing, absolutely nothing would come between her and this project.

Especially not an ex-fiancé who looked even sexier now than he had when she'd been head over heels. Too bad he had a cocky attitude and an overinflated ego.

Tamera was still seething that evening when she drove her silver BMW through the wrought-iron gates of her father's Coral Gables home. But by the time she'd pulled up in front and walked up the concrete steps, she'd forced herself to calm down.

Her father didn't need to know she was working with another firm right now. He especially didn't need to know it was Cole's firm. All he needed to do was concentrate on having pain-free days…if such a thing existed at this point.

She was certainly glad she'd calmed herself when her father's nurse came from his room with a grim face.

Panic coursed through her. "Danita, what is it?"

The elderly lady gripped Tamera's arm and led her to the living room. "I'm afraid it's time, Miss Stevens."

Tamera knew this day was coming. The day when remaining at home would no longer be a possibility for her father. Hospice was, of course, her next step.

She nodded. "I'll do what needs to be done, then. I just want him as comfortable as possible."

Danita offered a sad smile and squeezed Tamera's arm. "I'll talk to the doctor and see if there's any way we can keep him sedated here until the time comes."

For him to die. The sentence wasn't completed, but the words hung in the air just the same.

"I'd rather he be home," Tamera thought aloud. "But, if the hospice center can take him now, I will make those arrangements myself. I just signed on with a huge project at work, so I won't be able to take time off, but I will get him whatever he needs. I want him to be as comfortable as possible."

Two months ago her father was running one of the top architectural firms in the country and now he was struggling just to hang on. For her.

Tamera knew he had no reason to go on other than to make sure she was happy. And knowing how stubborn he was, he was probably hanging on to make sure she didn't screw up his company.

The idea made her smile through the pain. She wouldn't put it past him.

Seriously, though, she had to get this project drawn up. She had to contact Cole and make this happen sooner rather than later so she could give her father one last gift.

He could go in peace knowing she'd carry the torch that was passed down to her. He could rest assured she would go on to build amazing structures, and live up to the reputation her grandfather had fought hard to achieve for the company.

Tamera eased the door open to her father's room, careful to be quiet in case he was sleeping. No such luck.

She pushed the door open and stepped into the sunlit room. "I thought I'd find you asleep."

Walter Stevens turned his attention from the floor-to-ceiling window overlooking the bay toward her. "I didn't expect you today."

They went through this at every visit and every time she just laughed. The doctors said his mind would slip with this disease, but she didn't believe so. He was still just as sharp as he ever was. He was only testing her because he felt she should live in her office...as he had.

"What can I get you?" she asked, coming to stand beside the high-backed headboard of his bed, which was full of plump pillows. "More water or a snack? Danita is making dinner, but it won't be ready for another hour or so."

He waved a frail hand in the air. "You two worry too

much about me. Tell me about what's going on with the firm."

"We're moving forward and so far, so good. No one has asked too much about your absence because they're satisfied with the explanation that you're not fully retired, just practicing to see if it fits."

Once upon a time, he would've picked up on the fact that she'd danced around the question and eased into another topic. But that was when he was on his game and not fighting for every day he had left to live.

There was no way she was going to talk to him about the deal with Victor Lawson. He would only worry about details she had under control instead of his own health. She didn't want him to worry about anything.

Added to that, if she went into the details of the Lawson project with him, she'd have to add that they were paired with Cole's firm. She didn't want to have to explain that. Considering Tamera had cried herself to sleep for months and her father held her hand most of those nights, she doubted Walter would want to hear anything about Cole Marcum.

The project was best left out of the discussion. At least for now.

"I'm sorry all this is on your shoulders, Tamera. Work must be stressful," he told her, studying her face. "You have dark circles under your eyes. You're not taking care of yourself."

Offering her father a smile, she patted his arm. "No worries. I've got it all under control. I'm just getting used to filling the big shoes you left me."

He didn't chuckle at her half-hearted attempt to lighten the moment. "What aren't you telling me?"

She shook her head. "Nothing you need to worry about right now."

"I'm going to worry as long as I'm drawing breath," he assured her. "We haven't lost any clients, have we?"

"Of course not. All the clients, old and new, are pleased with the work we are providing. Now, quit worrying and just concentrate on yourself. I'm in charge now."

Finally, he smiled. "I bet you've waited a long time to say that to me."

"I have." She grinned back, though she hated that he was more like the child now and she the parent. "I'm going to go so you can rest before dinner. I'll call or come back later."

She kissed her father good-bye and let herself out of his Coral Gables estate to head toward her condo in South Beach.

SoBe was such a beautiful, tranquil setting. Maybe one day she'd get to enjoy the fashion shops and nightlife like she used to. She missed dancing, having fun with friends. But priorities came first, and going out mingling in celebratory style seemed inappropriate these days. No wonder she didn't have a love life or someone to support her during tough times. She hadn't been anywhere in what seemed like forever.

A stab of envy jabbed her as she passed the people milling about in and out of the specialty shops, strolling along the beach, laughing. Their lives seemed so carefree, so full of joy.

Tamera allowed the tears to fall, considering she was alone. She figured she was more than entitled. Her emotions had taken hit after hit today.

With the beginning of this project and the ending of her father's life, Tamera didn't know if she could take on an attack from Cole. But, if she could get her crying jags out in private, maybe she could put up a steelier front in public. Vulnerability and weakness had no place in her professional life.

When she pulled into her garage, Tamera pulled her cell from her purse. She dialed Cole's office line, fully expecting to get voice mail, but his strong voice came through the receiver.

"Cole Marcum."

She closed her eyes, rested her head against the leather headrest and swallowed the tears. "I didn't expect to get you this late."

"Tamera." His surprise, and smile, came through the phone. "Then why did you call?"

"To leave a message. I'd like to meet first thing in the morning to start on this design."

"Wonderful. My yacht is at Bal Harbor."

Her eyes flew open as she jerked upright in her seat. "Your *yacht?*"

"Yes, that's where I do my work. It's a place I can clear my thoughts and stay focused without interruptions. I will inform the staff they have the day off."

Tamera massaged her forehead, easing away the start of a tension headache. "I'm not having a meeting on your yacht. This isn't a social call, Cole. We're architects. We meet in boardrooms."

He chuckled, which only added to her already frazzled nerves.

"Tamera, that's how I work at the start of a project. I'll have a lunch prepared so we can just keep working. Besides, didn't Victor say to step outside the box? We can't go against our client's wishes, now can we?"

She resisted the urge to hang up on him. Clearly he was hell-bent on proving this was the only way to go.

"Trust me," he continued in that condescending tone. "You'll like the fact there will be nothing to worry about except how fast your Sharpie can keep up with that creative side I know you have."

Now Tamera laughed, shaking her head. "I'll overlook the fact that you just asked me to trust you and simply warn you that if you even attempt to charm me or toy with me the way you did earlier, I'll walk off that boat and we'll continue every meeting *inside* the box of my office. Now, which yacht is yours?"

He gave her specific directions and by the time she hung up, Tamera felt like she'd let control of this whole situation slip through her grasp. But if Cole did indeed work this way and Victor thought it would aid in the design process, she had to accommodate these men in order to get the blueprints done before…

Tamera stepped from her car and attempted to quickly resurrect some walls around her heavy heart. She couldn't take another beating. Not now when so much was on the line.

Three

Cole hadn't lied when he'd told Tamera he did his best work on his yacht, though if he'd been asked to work with any other firm, he certainly wouldn't have invited them on board.

He needed her to see more of who he was today. Not only that, he wanted to get this seduction plan rolling right off the bat. This was the perfect opportunity to kill three birds with one stone.

In their recent meetings, he hadn't missed the way her pulse leapt beneath that smooth, creamy skin on her neck, nor had he missed the way she moistened her lips as if she were nervous, aroused, or both. She wanted him as much as he wanted her and that angered her more than she cared to admit.

She wanted distance from him, which was understandable considering how he left things so long ago, but that wasn't the main reason she was moving away.

If her voice hadn't shaken, he may have just believed the flames shooting from her glare were directed in a negative way. But as he'd closed the distance between them, her words trembled.

Point for him for getting back under her skin in such a short time.

Reading a woman's body language was second nature to him and he'd had plenty of experience reading Tamera's. He knew her on every level a man and a woman could know each other. True, eleven years may have passed, but she hadn't changed that much. She was torn between wanting to see if their chemistry still existed and wanting to rip his eyes out.

Cole couldn't wait to see which power prevailed.

He was certain of one thing, though. When he wanted her, he'd have her. Seducing her would be no problem.

Tamera still had heat and desire, even if both were fueled by anger and rage. Her passionate side still existed and he was going to take full advantage.

"Hello?"

Tamera's voice echoed down through the galley. Cole put on his game face and stepped up onto the gleaming cherry finish of the deck. He briefly stopped in his tracks, forcing himself to act like a professional and let this physical attraction play out.

She was wearing a white skirt, simple white tennis shoes and a blue-and-white-striped sleeveless top. With her pale hair in loose waves around her shoulders, she looked so innocent. If only she knew where his thoughts had traveled.

"Come on down," he motioned for her to join him below. "I had the staff prepare some pastries and fruit. There's also a variety of juices."

He moved over to the kitchen and helped himself to a grape.

"Nice yacht."

Her sarcastic tone had him looking back over his shoulder. "Thanks."

"I never expected to see my name on the side of it."

Cole shrugged, refusing to rise to her challenge or mocking attitude. "Not your name. I named my boat "TAM" after the first stock I invested in that turned over a nice profit and allowed me to purchase such a luxury."

She eyed him as if she didn't believe a word he said.

"Oh, you thought I named it after you?" he laughed. "How awkward. But, seriously, I'd have a whole fleet if I named boats after all my exes."

He turned back to the fruit, ignoring the hurt in her eyes, not caring what she thought. He wasn't lying. Though he didn't tell her he invested in that stock because of her.

He was over what they had. Too much time had passed for him to still be harboring feelings for someone he'd cared about over a decade ago and he had too much on his plate these days anyway to keep someone like Tamera entertained in a relationship-type setting.

All he wanted from her was two things: design and sex.

He readied a plate for her and watched from the corner of his eye while Tamera stood in the entryway taking in her surroundings. His pride swelled. He knew how his cruiser yacht appeared—expensive and elegant.

"This is nice, Cole." Her tone had softened.

The surprise in her voice both irritated and pleased him. Growing up with nothing and working your way to the top did have advantages, but hadn't he told her he'd never have to scrape by again? Hadn't he said those very same words to her father? Hadn't he promised Walter Stevens that Tamera would never want for anything if Cole could marry her? Did she not think he could do it?

Obviously he had been the only one with faith in himself. Now he was even more irritated that he was second-guessing the past and replaying it over and over in his head.

"Yes, it is."

Reining in these emotions was the best approach right now. He had to keep the past out of their conversations and simply do what he told Zach—work on the design, and make Victor Lawson the happiest client and hotelier in the world. If anything happened with Tamera on an intimate level, well, he would consider this project a smashing success.

She placed her black briefcase on the table in front of the sofa. "I was running late and didn't get a chance to grab breakfast. That fruit is calling my name." She took a strawberry from the plate Cole offered her.

Cole reached for another grape, popped it in his mouth and stared. Was she really going to go on like there was no history? Like there was no sexual tension? Like they were just colleagues meeting for the first time?

Fine. That was just fine. He could work with this. The fact that she hadn't looked him in the eye since she'd stepped on board was just another positive in his favor. Her nerves were getting to her and he'd most definitely use that to his advantage…in business and pleasure.

"Do you want to sit on the sofa or at the dinette?"

She looked around the cozy living area. "The sofa will be fine for now since we're not actually drawing anything out. I think we need to brainstorm and then I can draw up some rough sketches."

Cole took a seat near her on the sofa.

She pulled papers from her briefcase and moved the case to the floor at her feet. He couldn't help when his eyes tracked her movements and he locked in on her small, tanned ankles against the stark white shoes. Nor did he feel guilty about reacquainting himself with her body all over again.

She was so delicate he wanted to run his hands up her petite legs to see if she still trembled beneath his touch. He wasn't delusional, though. Cole knew when he got his hands on her again, she wouldn't be the only one trembling. But this time, Cole wouldn't get his heart tangled in such a mess as love…or anything that remotely resembled that useless emotion.

"I assume you've had a chance to glance over everything," she said, reaching for another strawberry and biting into it.

Cole nodded and focused on the Lawson project instead of her full, pink lips making an O shape around the fruit. "Yes. It'll be an exciting ride, but well worth it, not only to our companies, but to the economy in Miami as well."

"I agree." She swallowed and pulled a paper from the folder. "I went through and categorized Victor's ideas."

Cole laughed, easing back into the corner of the beige leather sofa. "I remember you used to group everything. That was one of the things I lo—"

He shook his head at the major slip-up, and before he could backpedal, Tamera spoke up.

"We share a past, Cole. It's bound to come up at some point." She pointed to the sheet. "But as I was saying, I broke this down into groups. Necessities are marked in yellow, structure is in green, safety features are in red, décor is in pink. I saw Kayla's name on the contract. Is she working with you and Zach?"

Cole nodded. "She usually does all the décor for our projects. Actually, my sister is really anxious to get started on this. She's finishing up a project in L.A. right now."

Tamera tilted her head, causing her soft blond hair to swing over her shoulder. "Does she do independent work as well, though?"

"Yes, but the project she's doing now is for an office building Zach and I designed. She should be home in a couple of days."

Tamera's blue eyes sparkled. "I can't wait to see her again."

Not only had the Cole/Tamera tie been broken, so had the Tamera/Kayla bond. All because Walter Stevens had a chip on his shoulder and wanted better for his little girl than "trailer trash."

Tamera's soft, soothing voice slid over him as she talked about various groups she'd outlined. Cole listened, but only halfway. Her voice always did have that hypnotic effect on him.

Back at the University of Florida, Cole always found himself trying to study with her in her studio apartment and the next thing he knew they were naked and tangled in each others arms on the couch, floor, wherever.

When they stayed at his dorm, they always had to deal with Zach and his revolving door of women. That made evenings awkward for all parties involved, so they tended to stay at her apartment. It was amazing either of them made the good grades they did.

"Did you zone out on me?"

He shook aside the pleasant memories from what seemed like a lifetime ago and saw that she was smiling. "Just thinking ahead to the finished design."

She reached for another strawberry. "Tell me what you've been thinking as far as the theme for the hotel."

This was a no-brainer for him. "Classic. Timeless. Something from an era when life was simpler, women were elegant and men were gentlemen."

Her smile widened. "We're on the same page, then, because that's exactly the vibe I was getting from Victor's requirements and ideas."

"He knew we'd make a good team."

Damn. Admitting that in his head was one downfall he didn't appreciate. Having it out in the open was even more fatal to his position. He'd never let a woman have control over his emotions since Tamera and he'd be damned if he'd let her have that privilege ever again. Though the breakup was no fault of hers, the whole situation left a bitter taste in his mouth.

Tamera's baby blues stared as her smile faltered. Cole didn't say another word, but he could practically see the wheels spinning inside her head and those thoughts bumping into each other in her mind had nothing to do with business.

"This is going to be harder than I thought." She came to her feet, tossing the folder onto her vacated seat on the sofa. "I knew the past would come up in conversation, I just didn't expect it to be this uncomfortable."

Her declaration surprised him and he got up, too, standing almost toe-to-toe with her. "Look, if you can't handle this, you should've told Victor before you signed."

She shoved her shoulders back. "I can handle this just fine. I said it was uncomfortable. That's all."

"Really."

"Yes. Really. I mean to see you after all this time and then to act like this is a typical job. Not to mention the fact this is my first project as CEO."

"Congratulations, by the way," Cole offered, in an attempt to lighten the mood. "Didn't know your father retired."

He hated thinking of her father, but he hated even more when all color drained from her face at the mention of the man.

What the hell?

"Tamera?" Cole reached out to take her arm. "What's wrong now?"

She shook her head. "I'm fine. I don't want to disappoint my father and I don't want to let the firm down. I just have a lot riding on this."

No, there was something much more than that. Cole knew this woman well enough to know when she was holding something back, and she definitely was. Now he just had to figure out what was going on with Walter Stevens. She'd been fine until the mention of her father's absence. Odd that Cole hadn't heard of his retirement before. Was the man indeed retired or was something wrong?

She went on to say, "I'd actually like to work on this as much as we can to finish up the drawing as soon as possible."

"Not a problem." Why was she so rushed, he wondered, releasing her arm. "The sooner we get this done, the sooner we can start construction and hopefully get done before the projected date."

"That would be amazing."

"If you're so nervous about letting people down, why don't you just ask your father for advice? I'm sure he'd be more than willing to help you, especially since he just turned over the reins to you. He may even consider coming back for such an important project."

Walter would do anything for his baby girl, Cole thought, including threaten her fiancé and not give a damn he was hurting his precious daughter in the process.

Oh, but the thought of going toe-to-toe with Walter again got Cole's blood pumping. The image of the two of them being paired on this project was laughable and Cole found himself actually wanting the opportunity to present itself so he could show the old bastard what he was made of.

Tamera turned her back to Cole, her head drooping between her shoulders. "I really can't talk about my father, Cole."

Seriously? Something was definitely wrong.

Had something happened? Had he threatened Tam about this project? Surely not. But what had her so upset?

"Tam."

To hell with their past, present, future. To hell with the designs and his promise not to charm her. He needed to at least appear concerned. How else would he get her where he wanted her? He needed her to trust him, especially now, so he could get to the truth about Walter's real reason for being a no-show on the biggest project his firm had ever seen.

Cole placed his hands on her slender shoulders, squeezing gently when she only tensed.

"Whatever it is, push it aside. We can't allow personal emotions to interfere with this project."

When she turned back around, her eyes were misty, but that defiant chin was tilted. And because he didn't want her to mistake his touch for anything intimate, Cole removed his hand.

"It's just personal," she said, looking up. "Nothing I can't handle. I've just got more riding on this deal than you will ever know."

As if he didn't have a great deal riding on this project himself? The reputation of his firm was on the line.

"But I am begging you," she added. "Please don't make me stroll down memory lane with you. I just can't. I don't have the energy to fight you about it, either. Not now."

Cole nodded. "You have my word."

A mocking laugh escaped her. "That means nothing to me. Just concentrate on business."

More and more intrigued at what plagued her, he let her go, but knew without a doubt that whatever was hurting Tamera this much had to be something major. For her to give in to her emotions and nearly break down in tears in front of him told him that this strong woman was teetering on the edge.

Four

"Sleek, yet bold and elegant."

Tamera nodded, adding, "Old World elegance."

"Perfect."

Working in Cole's million-dollar yacht, earning high praise and approval from him shouldn't make her feel warm and tingly like a schoolgirl, but it did just the same.

Between her father's illness and the stress of trying to perfect the one design that could be the biggest career move she'd ever taken, she'd gladly embrace all the warm feelings she could muster…even if they came from the only man who'd taken her heart, squashed it and handed it back without even so much as an apology.

Cole eased back into the leather club chair and crossed his ankle over his knee. "Tell me more of your vision."

Tamera pulled out her black Sharpie and a sheet of

butter paper and laid it across his long, glossy dinette table. "Since this is Miami, we need to continue with the white stone, column and arched look, but keep it in the massive size." She drew some quick sketches, then stopped with her marker hovering over the sheet and closed her eyes. The finished product floated through her mind. "We want this to be grand like in *Casablanca*. Refined. Maybe not so much glitz, but all of the glamour. Polished."

"There should be two wide sets of stairs facing opposite directions, coming together as one and then leading up to the arched, open doorway of the resort entrance. Large pillars, maybe covered with greenery or flowers trailing over them at the base of the staircases with oversize, lantern-type lights."

"Stunning."

Tamera jerked upright, opening her eyes. Cole stood directly beside her, mere inches away. His heavy-lidded gaze roamed over her face, pausing on her mouth.

"All of it."

Tamera licked her lips and cursed herself when the innocent gesture sent the muscle in Cole's jaw ticking. The last thing they needed was more sexual tension. Hadn't he given his word *not* to rehash the past? Granted he wasn't saying anything, but his actions were purposely throwing her back to a time she couldn't settle into.

"Tell me your visions." She'd force him to be professional. But if he didn't step back, she was in danger of getting swept away by that intense gaze, by his amazing masculine cologne.

"Clean, crisp. Flawless."

"We're on the same page then. I'll draw up some more rough sketches in the morning and get with you in a couple of days. I'll call your assistant and set up another time to meet."

Placing her lid back on the marker, Tamera turned fully in an attempt to gather her things, but ended up bumping Cole in the process. He hadn't offered her room to maneuver, so now he was within inches of her face.

Wonderful. Not only did he have that sexy stubble on his face, those wide shoulders blocked her view of anything behind him. That darn cologne of his surrounded her just as if he'd wrapped his arms around her and pulled her against his broad chest. And, heaven help her, she knew precisely how those strong arms felt.

"I have everything on board to do rough sketches. My scale is in the desk." Though he didn't offer to move to get it. "No need to leave."

She looked him dead in his navy-rimmed eyes. "We both know there is."

"If you're uncomfortable—"

"Uncomfortable?" Tamera raised a brow and propped her hands on her hips. "I'm not uncomfortable. What I am is a professional."

A corner of his mouth kicked up, mocking her. "And you're implying I'm not."

She merely shrugged, moved around him and went to pick up her bag. But before she could make it back to the sofa, Cole's hand closed around her bare arm.

"Let's just get this out of the way." He spun her around to face him, his grip tight. "The Marcum Agency has an impeccable reputation, which is what landed us this job. I have never been, nor will I ever be anything less than professional. I'll admit working with you is difficult— I'm human and I'm male and you're still damn sexy. I can't help the fact I'm still attracted to you.

"Now, do I plan to act on my ill-timed feelings?" he continued, still holding her arm. "No. But I won't try to pussyfoot around the topic either."

Tamera refused to lick her lips, swallow or allow her gaze to travel from his eyes. She would not give him anymore ammunition to add to this awkward moment or his power over the situation.

She knew she needed to regain control, but nearly laughed at the irony. This was all they'd ever fought about before…control. Some things, bad as she hated to admit it, never changed.

"If you think I'm still attractive, that's an issue you'll have to deal with." Even if the idea made her tingle, he was still a cold-hearted, selfish jerk. "I'm not here to do anything other than work. I have too much going on in my life, even if we didn't share a past breakup, to pursue anything with anyone."

Again, he studied her face. Why did he feel the need to do that so much?

She jerked her arm free. "I'll have my assistant call yours."

Before he could call her back or get hold of her again, Tamera grabbed her bag, raced up the short stairs to the deck and onto the dock. Any more of those long, not-so-innocent looks or touches would send her up in flames. Because, like it or not, Cole Marcum was sexier now than she'd ever dreamed possible—and she had dreamt of him over the years. His professional status and standings only added to that sexy, exotic allure he had.

Why did fate have to mock her? Why did this person have to come back into her life at this point in time when she was most vulnerable? If he kept insisting on touching her, she might just give in to her desires and let him. Would he act so cocky then? If she surprised him and told him to take what he wanted, would he?

Just once she'd like to feel strong arms around her. Arms that would embrace her and lift all her heavy baggage and burdens. Arms that belonged to a man who loved her and cared whether she was happy or miserable.

But those were dreams she'd given up on long ago. If Cole offered her anything, it would be nothing beyond lust and she just didn't have the time or the energy to deal with uncomfortable emotions.

Since they were inevitably going to be spending time together, why couldn't she take what she wanted? Yes, she and Cole shared a past and were two different people now, but there was still that sexual pull. Even she couldn't deny that.

Tamera flew through the streets toward her condo and plotted. Yes, if Cole kept insinuating they should explore this passion that still lingered, she'd call his bluff.

Then they would see who held all the power.

"I'll come by and sign the papers tomorrow."

Cole stood in Tamera's office doorway and waited for her to acknowledge he was here. He leaned against the door frame, listening as she chatted away on the phone.

Beauty personified. Her head was tilted back against her leather office chair, the gesture exposing her creamy skin from her chin to the deep V in her silk blouse. Her silky blond hair was piled on top of her head in a sexy, messy way that only added to her appeal.

She held the phone to her ear, rubbed her forehead and sighed. "I want this to be as painless for him as possible."

Who? Obviously this was a personal call. All the more intriguing and all the more reason he should continue his ill-mannered eavesdropping.

Could this be the secret he'd wanted to discover about Walter or was there another man in her life? Too bad. He wanted this woman back in his bed. Now. Another man would just have to back down because he sure as hell wasn't going to.

"I appreciate all your help. Yes, I'll be fine. We knew this was going to happen, but knowing it and following through are two separate things. See you first thing in the morning."

Cole cleared his throat and righted himself as Tamera eased forward in her chair to hang up the phone. Had she known he'd listened in on much of a personal conversation, she'd blast him for his rudeness and expect an apology. Something he wouldn't dream of.

"Still believe in working overtime, I see."

He stepped into her office, and though he wasn't sorry he'd snuck up on her and listened when he really had no right, he was sorry for the shadows under her eyes and the turmoil broiling behind those beautiful baby blues.

"How did you get in?" she asked, coming to her feet.

"Your assistant let me in on her way out." He crossed the plush, white carpeting to stand on the opposite side of her glass-topped desk. "I told her we had a meeting scheduled late."

Tamera crossed her arms over her silky green shirt. The innocent gesture did absolutely amazing things to her chest, but that was definitely a thought he'd have to keep to himself.

"We don't have a meeting," she countered with a lift of one perfectly arched brow.

"We can," he said with a smile, hoping to take her mind off the intense phone conversation. "Let's go grab something to eat."

"We're not dating."

No, he didn't want anything that complex. "It's dinnertime and we can do some more brainstorming and combine our plans."

She searched the length of his body and back up. Again, the innocent gesture thing was killing him.

"I don't see your plans."

"They're in the car." He offered her another smile. "You coming or not?"

With a sigh, Tamera held her hands up in surrender. "All right. I have a few sample designs on my laptop. Tell me where we're going and I'll meet you there."

"I'll drive."

She eyed him, but Cole held her stare. No way was he going to let her get behind the wheel. She looked stressed, exhausted and ready to drop.

Seducing her into his bed would be so easy.

His body literally ached for that close contact again. But how could he take advantage of her in her condition?

Damn, why did he have to be such a gentleman at times? Especially when she obviously didn't even appreciate the fact.

"Fine, but don't think this is anything other than business." Tam came around her desk, crossed to a small closet tucked in the corner of her office and pulled out her bag. "Pull your car around front. I'll meet you there."

She followed him to the double glass front doors,

unlocked them and let him out. Even though she had no clue about his ulterior motive of getting her into his bed, Cole knew she wasn't stupid. She had to know that a chemistry as strong as what they had never fully disappeared, no matter how much you want it to.

God knows he'd thought she'd evaporated from his mind. But since the moment she'd breezed into the boardroom at Victor's office, then froze in her tracks at the site of him, she'd occupied more space than he cared to admit.

Liquor, women, fast cars, power and money had gone a long way in helping him recover from the damage Walter Stevens had done, the hurt he'd caused.

Granted, Tamera's father gave him an ultimatum of losing his scholarship or losing Tam. Had Cole had the funding to continue college on his own, he would've told the old man where to stick it, but since Cole, Zach and Kayla were all going to school on scholarships, he couldn't risk it. Not when they had absolutely nothing to fall back on but the old, run-down house their grandmother had raised them in after their parents' untimely death in a car accident.

Cole tapped the remote and his luxury SUV chirped as he unlocked it. As he slid behind the wheel he thought back to the days immediately following their breakup. He'd been purposely cruel so she wouldn't try to come after him or beg, because God knew if she'd begged he would've said to hell with school and the scholarship. Though there were countless times he'd wondered if he should've done just that.

But, in the end, how could he complain? He'd built, from the ground up, a multimillion-dollar business with Zach and Kayla. Without Walter's brash actions, he may not have been as successful and powerful.

And now that he held the power, he could hold the woman.

Cole pulled in front of The Stevens Group where Tamera stood in her classy emerald green, button-down shirt and slim gray skirt stopping at her knees. The soft Miami breeze sent loose strands of her hair dancing around her shoulders.

He swallowed. Hard.

Bombshell or not, he'd still made the right decision in giving her up.

Five

She should've known he'd choose the flashiest, most expensive restaurant in South Beach. Not to mention one that needed reservations at least a month in advance. Of course, once he flaunted his billion-dollar smile, the cute perky hostess, who may have been all of twenty, promptly seated them.

Cocky jerk always got what he wanted.

"We could've done this in my office," Tamera stated as she slid into the semi-circle booth in the back corner of the restaurant.

"We could've, but I'm hungry and if your habits are like they used to be, you skipped lunch."

Tamera froze, clutching her slim laptop case. "Stop trying to reminisce. You bring up the past every time we're together. We dated, you broke up. I've moved on."

Cole reached across the table, took her left hand,

examined her bare finger. "Doesn't seem like you have."

Fury bubbled through her as she jerked her hand away. "My personal life has no place in our conversation. You left me. Remember?"

She set the laptop on the edge of the table and unzipped the case. This had to remain a business meeting because if she even stopped to think about how his strong, smooth touch felt, she'd ask him to take her home.

How pathetic was that? The man had completely destroyed her happily-ever-after fantasy and her body still betrayed her. Whose side were her hormones on? His obviously.

Before he could comment, the waitress came and took their drink orders and offered fresh-baked rolls. Tamera booted up her laptop and tried to ignore the fact that Cole sat so close.

"Here."

She glanced up at a buttery roll all spread open and ready to devour. Cole smiled as he placed it on her saucer. Where exactly did he think his charms were going to take him?

"I can't concentrate on business if your stomach is growling," he commented, buttering his own steamy roll.

Once again he was seeing to her needs in small, subtle ways that made her want to ask what the hell happened to him all those years ago? Didn't she deserve some kind of detailed explanation? Didn't devoting nearly two years of her life to someone require some type of courtesy on his part when he made his exit?

"I hope that scowl isn't in regards to the design you're

about to show me," Cole said, drawing her thoughts back to the present.

She smiled sweetly. "My examples are flawless. My scowl is due to present company."

To Cole's credit, he kept his smirking mouth shut.

"Good evening."

Tamera glanced up to see Cole's twin, Zach, standing on the other side of the table with a leggy, busty blonde draped over his arm. The man was just as exotic-looking and handsome as Cole with dark eyes, dark skin and black hair. But Zach had always had a rougher, edgier side.

"Business meeting?" Zach asked, eyeing Tamera's computer.

"Yes."

Tamera thought it best to let Cole speak. There was no need to get back into that family any more than necessary. Though seeing Zach did bring back a flood of memories of a time when they all double dated with whoever Zach's love of the day was.

God, they were such different people then.

"The Lawson project?" Zach asked.

"It's the only project I'm concentrating on right now," Cole replied.

Zach's eyes roamed back to Tamera. "Good to see you again, Tam. How have you been?"

"Good, thanks."

She couldn't help but smile. Zach had been like a brother to her, though she could easily see why women wanted to be with him. The Marcum men were irresistible.

"I'll let you two get back to work." He turned and whispered something to his date, which prompted a high school-like giggle. "See you in the office, Cole. Tam, it was a pleasure."

Zach led his date to an intimate table across the restaurant and Tamera couldn't help but wonder what it would be like to be a woman who didn't allow her emotions to get all tangled up in a man. What would it be like to just let the moment take you away?

"That wistful look is much more pleasant than the scowl," Cole whispered in her ear. His warm breath tickled her shoulder through the thin silk blouse.

"Just taking a moment to daydream."

Cole rested his elbow on the table, not bothering to back away. "About my brother."

Tamera sighed and shifted to look Cole dead in his bedroom eyes. "Jealous? Fine. Since you're so hell-bent on rehashing this past between us, let's lay out all the cards."

The flash of surprise in his heated gaze gave her a brief moment of satisfaction.

"*You* ended our engagement," she began, refusing to allow the hurt or the anger to rise to the surface. "*You* wanted to move on for reasons you never explained to me."

Cole held up a hand, opened his mouth.

"No." She couldn't allow him to break her concentration with smooth words or useless excuses. "Your reasons don't matter to me now, they mattered then. If you are so concerned with what is going on in my personal life, just ask me. Granted, if I choose to answer you, you probably won't like what you hear. I've dated since you, Cole. I've even slept with some of the men I dated."

Okay, so she'd only been intimate a couple of times

since Cole, but he didn't need to know she was so pathetic she'd seldom had sex in eleven years.

"I'm sure you've been with women since me. It's life and it's the life you chose. So I'm done with your not-so-subtle stroll down memory lane. Can we please move forward now and work only on this project? I'm sure Mr. Lawson would appreciate that."

Cole smiled. He actually…smiled. "Your eyes still go ice blue when you get really angry. And it's just as sexy as ever."

"Did you not hear a word I just said?" God, the man could be so infuriating. Nobody else ever had the audacity to smirk at her after she'd confronted them. Then again, no one pushed her buttons quite the way Cole did.

"I heard you. But I should tell you something as well." He brushed a strand of her hair over her shoulder, leaned in and whispered, "I still want you. Business and past aside, you know you want me, too. I can see the desire in your eyes and don't think I haven't noticed how you bite your lip. You only do that when you're nervous or aroused."

Tamera jerked as if he'd hit her and the waitress chose that moment to come back to take their order.

"I'm not staying," Tamera informed the girl. "Cole, I'll call your assistant to set up another meeting. In my office."

Before he could say anything else, before Tamera's heated face gave away her true feelings, she snatched her laptop, case and purse and fled the restaurant. Zach and his date didn't even notice her abrupt departure because they were too busy forming one body in the corner of their booth.

Thankfully she'd driven here in her own car. There

was no way she could be in close quarters with Cole and his ego…there simply wasn't enough room.

Why did she have to find that confidence attractive? Had she not learned her lesson the first time? She did not need this added pressure right now, not with her father's health hanging by the proverbial thread.

Tamera slid into her silver BMW, set her belongings on the passenger seat and rested her head on the steering wheel. If she thought, for even a minute, that Cole had changed, that he could comfort her in the way she needed right now, whether in bed or out, she'd jump at the chance. To have strong arms envelop her, to rest her head on a set of shoulders that could carry her burdens, would be more of a turn-on than any charm he could throw her way.

But Cole wasn't offering anything that personal or intimate. Their versions of intimate were polar opposites and she just couldn't commit to his.

A sterile, stark white environment was not what Tamera wanted for her father's last days. Thankfully, the hospice nurse wasn't lying when she said the hospice facility was comfortable, less like a hospital and more like a home.

The private quarters were carpeted, and had small kitchens, beds and sitting chairs. Small chests of drawers and coffee tables with televisions completed the décor. Patients were free to bring personal items to feel more comfortable.

Regardless of the coziness, signing the papers to have her father put into strangers' care was one of the hardest things Tamera had ever done. Removing him from the home he'd made with her mother at the start of their marriage and placing him into hospice seemed like giving up.

But Tamera had to face reality. He wasn't going to get better so she may as well make his last days as comfortable as possible.

His cancer had spread throughout his body and there was no more the doctors could do. Some days his mind wasn't working as well as other days. He still knew who everyone was, but he would forget simple things like if the nurse had drawn his blood that morning or why he wasn't at home.

Nothing about this situation was easy and she had a dreadful feeling it was only going to get worse from here.

Tamera went from the nurses' station to her father's room to check on him one last time before she left for the night. Exhaustion had long since set in since she'd been back and forth all day bringing things from the house and making sure his room was set up to his liking. She'd do everything in her power to make him happy.

Thankfully he was asleep. Tamera clicked off the television and stood in the silence staring at the man who'd once made billionaire tycoons quake with fear. Now a pale, frail man, Tamera had a hard time believing this was her father.

Her throat clogged with tears. She'd give up all the money, houses, cars, yachts, everything in the Stevens dynasty if the cancer would just disappear.

After covering her father with his brown throw from his own bed at home, Tamera smoothed his thin hair from his forehead, kissed him and shut off the lamp.

This would be a good night. His medicine was strong enough to allow him the much-needed rest he deserved. These were the nights when Tamera caught up on her sleep as well. God knew she needed it now that she was dealing with Cole and Victor. She honestly didn't know which man scared her more.

Oh, who was she kidding? There was no contest.

With her hospice folder loaded with all her copies of the paperwork and her purse, Tamera waved goodbye to the nurses and stepped out into the unusual chill of the April evening. The somewhat crisp breeze seeped through her silky blouse, sending shivers all over.

She hated these odd Miami days. They were few and far between, but she'd stick with the days that were either hot or hotter. The folks up north could have this chill.

Tamera settled in her car, giving her body a moment to recover from the bitter wind she hadn't expected from Miami in April. As soon as she got home, she vowed, she'd change into her favorite lounge pants and long-sleeved T-shirt.

Driving through the streets toward her condo, she longed for home and a good book. All she needed was a steamy romance and a corner of her sofa where she could hopefully sweep her mind into a fictional life and leave the troubles of hers behind for a few minutes.

Unfortunately, as she pulled up, she saw one of her main issues sitting in his flashy, luxury car in her driveway. How many cars did the man have?

The sleek, black Lincoln could either belong to an FBI agent or a powerful CEO. She'd rather face the FBI.

Cole exited when she raised her garage door and pulled in. This was not what she wanted or needed. The last thing she could think about right now was the Lawson project or the fact that Cole had blatantly stated he wanted to sleep with her.

Tonight was *not* the night for her to give in and call

him on his threats. She didn't have the energy or the will to fight right now.

When Cole opened her door, Tamera gave in to the inevitable and gathered her folder and purse. He wouldn't leave until he came to say whatever was on his mind, so she may as well get this over with.

Tamera was shocked when she stepped from her car. Cole at least had a gentleman's knowledge to move back and allow her to ease out without brushing against him. Minor kudos to him.

He closed the door. "I called the office and they said you took the day off."

"Yes." Tamera stepped into her house through the door attached to her garage and slapped the button to close the garage door. She punched the six digit code to turn off the alarm. "I tend to do that at times."

Cole followed her inside, obviously intending to stay. "At a crucial time like this? I don't know about you, but I intend to work around the clock until this is perfected and turned in before Victor wants it. We need to put up a united front—"

"I had personal business," Tamera yelled, slapping her folder onto the central stone island in her kitchen. "Did you come here to criticize my work ethic or did you have a point you needed to make?"

Cole's eyes darted down to the folder and Tamera rushed to cover it with her purse. Too late.

"Who's in hospice?"

An exhausted sigh escaped her. "What do you want, Cole?"

His eyes darted back to hers. "Your father's in hospice."

Of course he'd guess. Cole wasn't stupid and her silence only validated what he'd surmised.

"I suspected something was wrong, but I had no idea." He took a step closer. "Why didn't you tell me?"

"And I should've told you why? You care? Or so you could use it against my company in the future?"

Too disgusted to look him in the eye, Tamera turned and marched through the open living space into her den. Habit had her settling into her wide window seat, grabbing a beaded throw and holding it to her chest, as if to hold in the pain, the hurt so Cole couldn't see.

She didn't want him here. Why couldn't he see that?

"You'd be surprised what I care about." Cole followed her into the cozy room and stood in front of her. "No matter how things ended between us, I don't want to see you hurt."

Bitterness over his soft words had her jerking her gaze up to his. "Then you better leave."

Six

If her bottom lip had quivered, if she had unshed tears, Cole would've left her to her emotional breakdown. But the fact that she tilted her chin in a defiant manner and the shadows under her eyes confirmed how exhausted she was, he couldn't leave her. Not like this. Not when she was on the verge of breaking and barely holding herself together.

Damn, he was always a sucker for distressed damsels, especially sexy, vulnerable ones. And as much as Cole hated Walter, he didn't want Tam this upset…about anything.

Cole eased down beside her on the window seat and fisted his hands in his lap when she turned to look out onto the lush, floral gardens.

When he'd called the office to get together to collaborate again on the rough sketches, he'd nearly gone into shock when her assistant said Tamera had taken a personal day.

But now he didn't know what he was more shocked at—the fact that her father was dying or that she'd done such a stellar job of hiding his condition from the world around him. Even Cole's assistant hadn't been able to uncover the reasoning behind Walter's untimely absence.

"How much longer does he have?"

"Not long."

At least she answered him, even if she wouldn't look at him. "And you're taking care of everything yourself, right? Including keeping his terminal illness a secret from associates and staff? Pulling long hours just to make sure the clientele doesn't catch on and to keep everything at the firm running smoothly?"

She swallowed and shook her head, sending a lone tear sliding down her cheek. He reached up and swiped her damp skin with the pad of his thumb, cupping her jaw with his palm.

Much to his surprise, she leaned into him.

How long had she been keeping this secret? How long had this burden been wearing her down and did her father ask her to go to all this trouble? Did he want her to bear the weight of such a large dynasty on top of the secrecy of his illness?

Walter Stevens' condition changed everything. Miami society in general would not be the same. This was news Zach and Kayla needed to know about as soon as possible. If any other bids came through the office, he needed them to keep an eye out. No way would he allow The Stevens Group to get ahead of him. Not now. Not when he could so easily take them over during this weak period.

If other contractors knew Walter Stevens was no longer running The Stevens Group, they would certainly think twice before submitting bids, no matter how formidable Tamera and her crew were.

Which begged another question: Just how long had Tamera been running the company? Obviously, she'd been doing a fine job, or there would've already been talk, but people in this business didn't like change and they didn't like being kept in the dark.

But once Walter died, how long would Tamera be able to keep this going? Perhaps buying The Stevens Group should be next on Cole's priority list.

Yes. Most definitely. Zach and Kayla would surely be on board with that plan.

"I hate this," she whispered, pulling back from his hand. "I hate my father being so fragile. I hate being in charge of his final days. And I hate that you came by tonight."

"I'm glad I did."

And he was. This useful piece of information would go a long way in boosting Cole and his firm beyond anything Tam's father could've fathomed.

"Is it so bad to lean on me for a bit?" He rubbed the tips of his fingers against his palm.

"I learned long ago not to lean on people."

The steel behind her emotions came through her tear-clogged voice. He didn't ask what time period she referred to. He'd let her down once and she wasn't so trusting anymore. He not only understood her point of view, he respected it. She was on her guard, which was probably safest for her in this case.

If she really knew that everything he was doing was because of the project and he was using that advantage to get her into his bed, she'd kick him so far from her home, he'd never see her in a personal setting again.

And now that he'd made the discovery about Walter, well, he needed to remain extra close to be ready to take over The Stevens Group when opportunity struck.

She needed to believe that selling was the only way… and that it was her own idea.

Speaking of what she needed, she needed to get out and enjoy all that Miami had to offer. A club near her condo in South Beach would be perfect. Perhaps a few drinks would relax her a bit and she could concentrate on herself and her needs.

She swiped her cheeks and Cole didn't hesitate to reach out, pulling her back against his chest.

"Relax," he crooned when she stiffened. "Don't read anything more into this than a friend helping you through a rough day."

"You're not my friend."

She may have protested with words, but her body slowly relaxed against his. Cole actually felt the tension leave her, starting with her shoulders, her back.

"Why are you doing this?" she whispered into the dimly lit room.

"You're hurting, Tam. Do you think I'm that cold-hearted?"

Silence stretched through the room for several minutes, but Cole didn't care, not when Tam felt so good against him. Her warm body only heated his that much more.

Her head tilted to the side, resting firmly against his heart. Her breathing slowed. She'd fallen asleep.

Cole smiled, settled his arms firmly around hers, which were wrapped around her abdomen. Having Tamera sleeping in his arms was sweeter than anything he could've planned. Dying or not, if old man Stevens could see them now, well, that would definitely do him in.

Eleven years ago he'd purposely hurt her to make her keep her distance. She'd cried then, too, but in that steely, I-hate-you way.

But, seriously, what did he expect when he'd delivered the "it's not you, it's me" speech? In reality, though, it *had* been him. If he'd come from money he wouldn't have had to worry about those blasted scholarships. Not only that, he'd had to worry about Zach's and Kayla's as well. He couldn't disrupt his whole family because of her father.

A moment which plagued every day of his life since. Not only did he not stand up for the woman he loved and what they shared, he didn't stand up for himself.

Pathetic. Cole hated thinking about how weak and powerless he'd been.

Now, there was no reason for Tam not to see him for the man he'd become. Holding her like this only made him want her more. He wanted to explore that sexual pull he knew still existed between them. Granted, her father may have sucked the romance and love right out of anything Cole knew, but the man couldn't change the fact that Tamera was sexier now than ever and Cole intended to have her.

Tamera stirred against his chest and sighed. When she woke, he'd discuss her needs and subtly force his way into her personal life. He needed to gain her trust once again if he was going to persuade her to sell the company. But he knew this plan teetered on a fine line. Tamera was a strong, confident businesswoman. Convincing her to sell would be quite a challenge.

Cole's eyes scanned her den. The spacious room

with all its little accessories and knickknacks was so Tamera, but Cole also got a sense for the woman she'd become.

The beaded lampshades and Persian rug were no surprise, but the small certificate hanging behind her desk did catch him off guard. She was a member of the "Make-A-Wish Foundation." Hanging next to the certificate was a card, obviously made by a child's creative hand. It depicted a smiley face at the end of a rainbow. Drawn on pink construction paper, the word "thanks" was written in all caps with a backward k.

His eyes scanned over to her selection of CDs, again giving him a glimpse as to the woman Tam was today. Back in the day she enjoyed country music and was ready to let her hair down. He only saw one country CD, Faith Hill. The others were a mix of jazz and light rock.

What had she done in those eleven years they'd been apart? Had she fallen in and out of love again? Had her father meddled in her personal affairs? All questions he wanted answers to, but knew he wouldn't get and didn't deserve. And, he asked himself, why did he care at this point?

Tamera stirred once again and started to sit up. "Cole?" she asked, her voice groggy. "What time is it?"

He glanced at her desk clock illuminated by a small Tiffany lamp. "Midnight."

She eased up, brushing her hair from her face. "I didn't mean to fall asleep on you."

"You needed the rest." When she tried to ease away, Cole tightened his hold around her waist. "Are you okay now?"

She nodded, looking him in the eye. "Why didn't you

leave? You could've left me lying in the window. I have taken quite a few naps here."

He smiled. "Wishing on stars?"

Tamera's gaze moved to the window. "Something like that."

"Sneaking out is for cowards. I face complications head-on."

She looked back at him, questions, hurt swirling in her eyes. "This isn't right, Cole. You really shouldn't be here."

"Because of what we're feeling? What isn't right about it?"

Her delicate hand came up to her forehead as she closed her eyes. "We're business associates, nothing more. I can't concentrate on my father, this project and you all at the same time."

"Then don't." He took her hand from her face and held it. "Concentrate on this."

In a possessive manner he took her mouth. Every fiber of his being wanted to claim her, take her in a fast, frenzied manner, but she needed to ease into this. She needed comfort and he would be the one to offer it.

Her lips parted beneath his and Cole knew everything they'd shared before was nothing compared to the intensity of this moment. In her den, her own territory, Cole knew Tamera could relax. The dim light, the hour, all worked together in his favor. No phone would ring, no one would disturb them.

This moment was all about giving in to the inevitable.

Cole released her hand and brought his up to frame her face as he changed the angle of the kiss. Tamera twisted her body so they were more in line, then slid her arms around his neck.

Tamera's need must've taken over because Cole's control slipped from his grasp and easily into hers. A controlling woman in an intimate setting was sexy personified.

The familiar taste and touch only added to the need swelling inside him. Tamera was the only woman who'd ever been able to pull that desire he'd kept so hidden to the surface.

Cole had to tamp a portion of that desire back down. All he had to give Tamera was here, now. He had nothing else to offer, and even if he did, their souls were too battered from the first encounter. Lust was all this was, all it could be. And he was fine with that. Actually, right now, he was feeling pretty damn good.

"No." Tamera eased back shaking her head.

"What's wrong?" Cole asked, though he knew that was a dumb question.

"This," she gestured between their faces. "I won't do this with you again."

"Tam, I'm not taking anything you aren't offering. Anything beyond this moment doesn't matter."

She looked him dead in the eye. "*Everything* beyond this point matters. You crushed me once. It won't happen again."

When she sprang to her feet, turning her back on him, Cole didn't stop her.

"Why can't you just go with what you're feeling?" Cole came to stand behind her, but didn't invade her personal space by touching her again. "I'm not looking for anything beyond right now."

A small, sarcastic laugh escaped her. "That almost makes it worse," she whispered. "Just go."

Those were the two words he'd been both waiting for

and dreading to hear. Cole was torn between wanting to stay to comfort her and giving in to her request.

"I don't want you to be alone when you're hurting."

She turned to face him, tears shimmering in her eyes. "Seeing you, touching you, that's making the hurt worse. This is too familiar, Cole and I just can't get involved with you on a personal level again."

"Too late."

"Cole, please. Don't."

Despite her plea, Cole reached for her, taking her by her shoulders. "This attraction won't go away, Tam, no matter how hard you push me away. Our past had nothing to do with that kiss."

She grasped his forearms, her fingers biting into his cotton shirt. "Do you enjoy pressuring me? You say you don't like to see me hurting, yet you're still here, still bullying your way into my life when I've tried to keep you out. If you're regretting the decision you made all those years ago, that's something you're going to have to deal with. But leave me alone."

Shoving him aside, Tamera walked back to her window seat and curled up with her throw pillow. Her rigid back, her gaze out onto the starry night, was all he needed.

She'd begged, she'd nearly cried, but her silence and stiffness told him he'd reached her breaking point. Tamera had her pride, something he could appreciate. He wouldn't make her break even more tonight. He'd pushed, she'd given what she could, which was more than he'd expected. But he would get nothing else from her right now. Soon, he vowed.

With a heavy heart for Tamera's hurt, and the

knowledge of her father's terminal illness, Cole let her be, retreating to plan his next course of attack on both business and personal levels.

Seven

"Yes, Mr. Lawson, Cole and I are moving quicker than we'd anticipated with the designs."

Tamera leaned back in her leather office chair and rolled her eyes. No need to add that Cole was moving faster than she'd expected with the personal side of things as well. Her lips still tingled, her heart still ached.

"I'm glad to hear it, Tamera," Victor said. "And please, call me Victor. I'd like to set up something with the three of us later in the week so I can see where we stand. I prefer to be very hands-on when it comes to my properties."

Already? God, now she would have to put in extra hours with Cole to get this design more definite. Wonderful. Just what they needed. Working together after hours with no one else around but the two of them. Perfect.

"I'll have my assistant set up the appointment," Tamera offered. "I will let Cole know. We are very eager to show you what we've come up with."

Yeah, so far they'd managed to have a meeting aboard Cole's yacht where they shared some ideas and a very rough design, a botched dinner where she'd barely managed to get her laptop out of the case and an impromptu meeting at her house which only led to a course of events she didn't want to think about.

"Thanks, Tamera. I'm anxious to see the initial design."

"See you next week."

Tamera hung up her phone and laid her head on her desk. Her plans were nearly completed, so perhaps she could just e-mail them to Cole. They'd pretty much collaborated together that first day at his yacht and decided on the main architectural design for the exterior. The interior was still questionable, but perhaps with a couple meetings this week they could decipher the exact layout.

But first a phone call needed to be made. Tamera picked up her phone and dialed.

"The Marcum Agency," Cole's cheery assistant answered.

"This is Tamera Stevens for Cole Marcum, please."

"Hold one moment, Ms. Stevens."

Not five seconds passed before Cole's low, rich tone came over the phone. "Tamera, what can I do for you?"

She shoved aside the bubble of arousal at his voice and gripped the receiver. "We need to have a business meeting tonight after work. We can meet here in my office. I will have my caterer bring in some food."

"I had plans tonight," Cole countered.

Tamera leaned back into her buttery leather chair and gritted her teeth. "Call her and cancel. We have work to do."

"Jealous, darling?" Mocking laughter reverberated back through the receiver. "I'm flattered."

The urge to throw the phone against the wall was strong, but she refrained from acting like a child. "I didn't call to stroke your ego, Cole. I'm sure your entourage of women do that for you. I called on a professional matter, not a personal one. So, call your... date and tell her you have other plans."

"Will you make it worth my while?" he laughed. "Just kidding, don't get all worked up again. I'll be at your office at six."

Without another word Cole hung up and Tamera cursed herself for sounding like a jealous teenager...and cursed him for mocking her. Why was it her business if he was spending the evening with someone else merely because he'd heated her up in her home last night? Hadn't she come to her senses and kicked him out?

There was no time for anything but work, not only on this project, but in her life. She just couldn't let her mind wander to Cole and what he did in his free time. She already had enough to keep her mind and heart occupied every waking minute.

Heart?

Great, now she was delusional enough to think her heart was getting tangled around this project just because she was working with Cole. Just what she needed.

Tamera asked her assistant to hold all her calls and show Cole in when he arrived. She also had her call the caterer they always used and order enough food that the two of them wouldn't need to leave the confines of her office for a very long time.

Closing all the documents on her laptop, Tamera then pulled up her design on the screen. She twisted her hair up into a clip and slid her reading glasses from her desk and plopped them on the end of her nose. Not the sexiest look—she was only thirty-three and needed cheaters—but work came before beauty.

She tweaked the exterior just a tad to showcase the expansive, arched entryways. Six ran along the front of the resort, separated only by wide marble columns. Yes, marble. Why hadn't she thought of that before for the entryway? A Mediterranean flare with Old World elegance…it would be breathtaking and well-received.

Because her mind had been on other things, that's why she hadn't thought of the obvious.

There needed to be large, trickling fountains both inside and out as well. The soothing effect would only add to the fantasy getaway.

Tamera slipped off her Gucci shoes and left them beneath her desk. Padding over to her easel, she pulled out the rough sketches she'd made before she'd received the contracts and was just wishing she'd get the bid.

The lighting wasn't quite right in her initial draft on her computer, but what she'd originally drawn seemed like a better fit. The tall tapered lights weren't too overbearing to take away from the scrolling wrought-iron stair railings and the carved marble trim above the columns, surrounding the sculptured ceiling.

Encased lights needed to be set above each arch to shine down on every opening as well. This resort needed to appear to be glowing from the water's edge, rising from the ocean like a dream come to life.

She hovered over her board, looking at all the other initial ideas she'd taken to paper. Sometimes your first instinct was the best decision.

"I left early."

Tamera spun to her doorway to see Cole striding across her office.

Okay, there was that exception to the rule about your first instincts. Sometimes they were way off base, especially where this man was concerned.

"What time is it?" she asked, straightening from her tilted board.

"Four, but I didn't have any meetings left today."

Tamera rubbed the soreness in her back and twisted from side to side.

"Kayla wanted me to tell you 'hi' and she hopes to see you soon."

Smiling at the image of Cole's younger, quiet sister, Tamera said, "Tell her to call or stop by. I'd love to see her."

Cole closed the space between them, spun her around, making her face away from him. Next thing she knew, his fist was rubbing at just the right spot in her back where the cramp was.

"I was having dinner with her tonight." His touch continued to scorch her through her thin, silk blouse. "That's who I had plans with."

"Oh."

Nothing else came to mind to say, not with his warm breath on her neck, his magic hand doing wonders for her achy back and certainly not with the memory so fresh of their kiss.

"Do you know what a picture image you made when I came in?" he whispered next to her ear. "Bare feet, all that golden hair piled on top your head, those sexy glasses perched on the end of your nose?"

Sexy glasses? The ones she continually referred to as her "cheaters"?

"You're lucky it was me and no one else." Cole turned her back around. "I've never seen a sexier sight."

His mouth came down so fast, so hard on hers, she didn't have time to think or to react in any other way than to wrap her arms around him and let him in.

God help her. She didn't think she could've stopped him if she'd even wanted to. And that really, really should be a red flag. Their level of intimacy was growing with each and every encounter.

Cole's hands covered her back as he wrapped her in his embrace and arched her body. The heat from his chest did amazing things to her sensitive breasts through her thin top.

He lifted his head, still keeping her dipped beneath him. "Don't ever tell me again that there's no attraction between us."

Abruptly Cole released her, causing her to nearly stumble back before she regained her footing.

Damn that man for heating her up twice in one day and making her forget her priorities. And what the hell was that little stunt? Was he mocking her? Making her doubly aware that, yes, she was turned on by him and, yes, he could probably still have her in his bed?

Tamera straightened her blouse back into place, smoothed a hand across her forehead to remove stray hairs and crossed to her desk.

From here on out, this meeting was going to be hands-off. The desk or a blueprint would remain between them at all times.

Or God help her, she'd probably give in to her desires and say to hell with it and let Cole have what they both wanted.

Eight

If she wanted an apology for his actions, she would be waiting a very long time. He hadn't had a choice in the matter. Not when he'd stepped into her office and seen her barefoot with bare legs stretching up beneath a slim skirt as she bent over her easel.

And, if that hadn't been enough to get his testosterone pumping, she'd spun around with those sexy gold-rimmed glasses and her hair pulled into some strange, yet ultra sexy mess atop her head.

Technically, she should be apologizing to him. Since the start, she'd tortured him with her sultry style, her innocent looks and her demanding persona.

In a fruitless attempt to let them both regain their bearings after that scorching kiss, Cole stepped over to her sketches she'd been studying.

"Looks good," he said as his trained eye ran over nearly the exact same design he'd constructed in his mind.

"I didn't ask for your approval," she snapped.

Her clipped tone had him glancing over his shoulder, but he wasn't foolish enough to grin. He'd gotten under her skin. Good, because she sure as hell had been under his since the second they'd been in the boardroom two weeks ago with Victor.

"I wasn't giving it. I don't know why, but I'm surprised at how much your drawing resembles my own."

She glanced around. "And where, precisely, is your design? You came here for a business meeting, not to paw me again."

This time, foolish or not, he did smirk as he turned to give this vivacious woman his full attention. "Paw you? Honey, I haven't even begun to paw. Just say when."

The growl that came from her throat as she spun toward her desk only made him laugh. "That wasn't very ladylike."

Tamera dropped into her seat. Back ramrod straight, she glared out of the corner of her eyes. "I'm not feeling ladylike where you're concerned."

Taking his time, he crossed the spacious office and leaned a hip on her desk. "Your drawings by hand are way better than anything I have on my computer. You always were the really artistic one."

She wiggled her mouse and clicked on her computer. "I have a more updated version on here. I actually find the drawing and plotting on paper relaxing and lately, I need that."

He understood all too well, though he wouldn't admit that to anybody but himself. And certainly not to Tamera.

Cole moved to look over her shoulder at the exterior she'd pulled up on her screen. "Perfect. That's exactly what we'd discussed. You've certainly captured Victor's visions."

She smiled, glancing up at him. "Thank you."

Cole swallowed a bitter lump as Tamera looked back at her screen, pulling up yet another new design. She'd genuinely smiled at him and all he did was compliment her work.

Obviously they were more alike than he'd wanted to admit. When a client or fellow associate complimented his work, nothing pleased him more. The bond with their work was something he hadn't considered.

Perhaps he'd been taking his approach with Tamera in the wrong direction. He needed to get to her through her business. Talking about designs could be sexy… couldn't it?

They were in Miami, for pity's sake. Miami was the sexiest city, as far as he was concerned. Wealthy, powerful people simply added to the allure. Besides, hadn't Victor himself required a sexy theme for his hotel? The client's needs always came first.

"The entryway?" he asked over her shoulder, getting back to the task.

Cole also had a feeling that staying focused would not only throw her off and make her want more, but she'd also find him more attractive. Now if he could just keep his hands to himself.

The things he did for the goals he wanted to achieve.

"Yes." She pointed to the blueprint on the screen. "High intricate ceilings with large chandeliers. I'm thinking three, but we'll leave that final call up to Kayla."

"Good idea," he laughed. "She hates when I try to move in on her territory."

Tamera clicked her mouse again and pulled up the first floor layout. "Here's where the offices, meeting rooms, sauna, gym and maintenance rooms will be."

"What about the ballrooms?" Cole asked, studying the draft.

She clicked again. "I've put them on the top floor to have access to the rooftop where I'm hoping Kayla will put a botanical garden of sorts. She does all the interior, but she's so great with gardening, I'd like her to take this on as well. I also added the courtyard, but, yet again, will leave those main details to Kayla and Victor. I'm sure she'd love to handle this aspect of the project as well."

Cole was amazed at all the detailed work Tamera had already done since they'd first met aboard his yacht... especially in light of her father's condition. Though he knew Walter's condition was precisely the reason she'd worked herself to death.

"I'll run that by her," Cole said. "Though I'm sure she's already thought about every single aspect of this project. She's just as eager as the rest of us to please Victor, though she's a little intimidated."

"There's no need for that. She's amazing." Tamera pulled up another screen. "Here is the first floor. I'm keeping this layout simple seeing as how Victor wants each room to feel more like a loft than a hotel suite. I've factored in twelve guest rooms on the first six floors and the eight middle floors will have larger suites with full kitchens. I've also placed the honeymoon suites on the top, three floors to give couples privacy and a wonderful view from higher up."

Cole eased back and stood straight up. "I'm impressed, Tam."

Swiveling around in her seat, Tamera smiled that

bright smile that had never failed to clutch his heart years ago. He'd better keep a tight hold this time. No way did he want anything that resembled a relationship or commitment.

But, seriously, how had someone not captured Tamera's heart in eleven years? Was she that caught up in the firm? That he could understand, but he still couldn't believe some man didn't make her take the time to enjoy life.

"Thanks. I was hoping you'd like what I did. I tried to follow Victor's instructions and add a few of my own ideas as well."

Cole nodded. "Now we just need to do some more detailed planning as far as structure setup."

A knock on Tamera's office door pulled him from his thoughts. Tam came to her feet, still bare, and crossed over the plush, white carpeting.

As she swung the door open, her assistant came in, wheeling a cart. Silver-domed plates on a three-tiered cart came to rest in front of Tam's desk.

"Thanks, Mariah," Tamera said. "You can go now. Mr. Marcum and I will be working late tonight. I'll see you in the morning."

Mariah smiled and nodded to Tamera and Cole. "Good night."

Once the assistant closed the door behind her, Cole's gut tightened. They would be alone for the rest of the night and he was supposed to concentrate on designs?

"This smells so good," Tamera commented, lifting off the lids. "I'm starving."

Cole nearly laughed. Starving, yeah, so was he.

He wished Tamera would just give in to the sexual pull she was fighting so he could focus on the biggest business deal The Marcum Agency had ever dealt with.

He'd hate to screw this project up for his brother and sister all because he couldn't control his adolescent hormones.

Tamera picked up a piece of fresh pineapple and sank her teeth in, groaning. Wonderful. Just wonderful. Groaning was certainly not going to help him concentrate or keep his lust levels under control.

God, had she just groaned? That was so not meant to slip out.

Tamera swallowed the bite of succulent pineapple and turned to Cole, who was eyeing her beneath heavy-lidded eyes. Damn, so he had noticed the groan.

"Help yourself," she gestured toward the spread. "We can set all the plates over there if you'd like."

She picked up the tray of fresh fruit and went over to her long, granite-topped table by the floor-to-ceiling windows in the corner.

Cole just wheeled the cart over and began arranging the plates. "Were you really hungry when you ordered or do you plan on keeping me here until the hotel is built and open for business?"

Eyeing all the food, she laughed. "Sorry, it all sounded so good at the time, but now that I'm looking at it, it is an awful lot."

Fresh fruits, peeled shrimp, her favorite veggie wraps, some bread with raspberry dipping sauce, wine.

Okay, so maybe she did want to keep Cole here, so what. She wanted the man on a purely physical level and there wasn't a thing wrong with that. Was there a woman alive who didn't appreciate broad shoulders, tailored suits, dark, exotic looks and an edge of cockiness?

Was it her fault her memory was good and she recalled all their nights together so many years ago? No.

She was a woman with needs. That didn't mean she had to act on them.

End of story.

"I had no idea you were a member of the Make-A-Wish Foundation."

Tamera glanced up as Cole reached for a wrap, handing it to her on a small square napkin embossed with the restaurant's logo.

"How did you know?"

"I saw the small card a child had made you hanging next to your certificate in your den."

Tamera's throat closed up. "Emily made that card for me two weeks before she died."

Cole eased down in a leather chair across from her. "I apologize for bringing up bad memories."

"It's okay. She was the sweetest little girl, though." Tamera recalled the frail six-year-old with bouncy blond curls and bright blue eyes. "She also called me Tam because my name was hard for her. She's the only person, other than you, who's ever called me that."

Cole reached across and placed his hand over hers. "You don't have to tell me. I was just caught off guard when I saw that picture."

"We met when the foundation called and asked for monetary donations. I never can resist helping children, so I took the check personally to the office and there was this little girl and her mother. The little girl looked so full of hope with her big blue eyes. Her mother, on the other hand, looked lost, sad.

"I immediately took to Emily and she to me, so I became more and more involved. She made me that card because the foundation sent her to Disneyland and I went with them. All she wanted was to meet Minnie Mouse." Tamera looked over at Cole, tears clogging her throat.

"Do you know what it's like to give someone such a simple gift, knowing there's nothing else they want? I could've bought Disneyland for her, but it wouldn't have changed the fact that she was going to die."

When a tear escaped, Tamera pulled her hand from beneath Cole's and swiped angrily at her face. "Sorry. I just get so worked up thinking how unfair it is that people have to suffer such a horrible disease while I go about my life making more money than I could possibly spend and living any way I desire."

"She had cancer, didn't she?" Cole asked, his voice low.

Tamera closed her eyes. "How did you know?"

"I assumed since you're still so torn up that it was hitting close to home for you right now."

Yes, it was. But rehashing the past and dwelling on the inevitable with her father was not going to get Victor Lawson's hotel designed and built.

And it certainly wasn't helping her situation with Cole. That chip on his shoulder seemed to disappear and make room for her when she needed to lean on him.

Tamera shook aside the glum thoughts. "Let's talk about the design, okay?"

Cole eyed her as if he wanted to say or ask something else, but in the end he nodded. "Okay."

But instead of approaching another topic, they ate in silence, for which Tamera was grateful. Cole obviously still could read her well enough to know when she needed space. He also probably still knew how much she hated being seen as vulnerable or weak.

Tamera feared, though, if he kept offering subtle support, she'd take him up on it…and then some. Thank God he hadn't. If she landed in his arms again, especially under emotional circumstances, who knows what would happen.

Oh, who was she kidding? She knew exactly what would happen and she was nearly to the point she didn't care.

Nine

"What about carrying out the columns throughout the hotel, even in the suites? That way the weight-bearing walls won't take up so much space and we can keep the rooms open for that airy feeling." Tamera's Sharpie moved in a quick, swift manner as she refigured some very rough sketches and glanced up to get Cole's reaction. "What?"

He'd shed his Italian jacket and silk tie just after they'd eaten and loosened the top two buttons of his cobalt blue dress shirt. And every moment since he'd done so, that golden skin peeking through the V of his open collar taunted her.

"I think you need to call it a night," he told her, his thick, dark brows drawn together in worry.

Tamera glanced to her glass desk clock. "It's only ten, Cole. We used to work well into the night when we were in college."

As soon as the words were out of her mouth, hovering in the air between them, she wished to snatch them back. She'd been getting on him about rehashing their past, and that was certainly a place she couldn't keep revisiting, but the statement just slipped through her lips.

"Maybe I'm getting too old for all-nighters," he commented.

Those deep brown, heavy-lidded bedroom eyes told her different. A determined man, a *powerful* man like Cole didn't think twice about pulling all-nighters… whether it be the bedroom or the boardroom.

Tamera rolled her eyes. "Please, you're not too old. That implies I'm old and I'm not."

He stepped forward, placing his hands on her shoulders and massaging the tension away stroke by delicious stroke. Mercy, the man did know exactly what to do when she needed something. She didn't even have to ask.

"You're still just as beautiful as you were, Tam," he told her in a low, sexy tone. "Age only improves you. But I do think you've reached your limit today. We can work more tomorrow."

Eyes closed, she leaned into his hands and enjoyed, just for a moment, what he was so graciously offering. His smooth words settled over her, giving her a brief sense of calm she so desperately needed, craved.

Why couldn't they be meeting for the first time? Why did all of her memories of this man come with an ache in her chest that she could never ease?

"Do you have plans this Friday night?" she asked.

His soft laughter filtered through her quiet office, making her even more aware of the fact they were in this massive building all alone. Even the janitor had left at eight.

His hands stilled on her shoulders as he leaned down to whisper in her ear. "You're the only plan I have."

Why did that threat sound so thrilling?

"Fine. We can meet here when you get off."

He began massaging once again. "No, we need a change of scenery to keep our creative juices flowing. Let's go back to my yacht. It's private, it's supposed to be a nice evening, maybe we can work topside under the stars."

Seduction. He was trying to seduce her. She was just intrigued enough to see his course of action. And, she had to admit, she enjoyed being on his yacht. It was quiet, and if the staff was off that day, there should be no interruptions.

"Would you offer this deal to just anyone that you'd be working with on a project like this?"

"What deal?"

Tamera turned in her chair, causing his talented hands to fall away from her shoulders. "Meeting, once again, on your yacht."

Cole shrugged, placing his hands in his pant pockets. "I'm not working with just anybody, Tamera, I'm working with you."

And that was the problem, she was starting to like working with Cole…a little too much for her comfort level. What was worse, she had a feeling he knew where her emotions were headed…straight to him no matter where he led her.

"I'll provide the food," he continued as if she'd already agreed to step into his web of deceit. "Just e-mail me all those files we worked on."

She studied him, seeing him for the young man she'd

fallen in love with. He'd shown so much potential to be a powerful CEO then. Of course, the man Cole was today was not exactly the man she'd envisioned.

She hadn't expected the cocky demeanor or the take-charge attitude where everything was his way or no way. But in the back of her mind, she still kept that vision of him as a husband, a father. He'd be just as powerful in running a family as he was running a multimillion-dollar company. What happened to make him so hard and brash the majority of the time? Every now and then, though, she appreciated, and was attracted to, those moments when he slipped back into the man she used to know.

"I'll make sure I'm at the yacht by five," he told her, moving around her desk to the club chair where his jacket and tie lay. "If there's any problem, just text or call me."

That was it? He was just going to leave without attempting to kiss her? After the whirlwind way he swept into the room he was going to exit without any fanfare?

Mixed signals, anyone? What game was he playing with her?

Tamera gestured over to the table where the spread of half-empty plates and silver platters full of fruit and wraps lay. "Do you want to take any of this food?"

"No. Why don't you save it for your lunch tomorrow? There's enough for your assistant, too."

Tamera smiled. "You make millions of dollars each year and you are worried about leftovers?"

His face sobered as his eyes captured hers. "No matter the amount of money I make, I still remember where I came from."

As if she needed another piece of her heart to melt

at this man with whom fate had mockingly reunited her. She couldn't get swept into another entanglement with him. Seduction was one thing. Sleeping with each other, if that's where this was headed, was one thing. Keeping her heart intact and to herself was a whole other matter.

"I'll make sure it doesn't go to waste," she promised. "See you tomorrow."

He walked back and leaned down so they were eye to eye. "Go home and get some sleep."

The way he loomed over her as she sat in her office chair made her feel uneasy, and even though he demanded instead of asking, she knew he was concerned.

"I'll be leaving in a few minutes."

"I'll wait to walk you out."

Crap. She'd wanted to do just a couple more things before she called it a night. But more than likely he knew she was lying, so that's why he called her on it.

"All right."

There wasn't a woman, no matter who she was and what she'd been through, who didn't want to be looked after, cared for, in some regard. If Cole wanted to make sure she didn't overwork herself and see that she got to her car safely, then who was she to put up a fight? A little white knight routine every now and then would go a long way in helping her get through this ordeal with her father.

"Let me get all the lights and my purse."

"I'll wrap up the food and put it away."

Tamera gestured. "The refrigerator is through those doors over there in my makeshift apartment."

Cole laughed as he dropped his jacket and tie back in the chair they'd just vacated and went over to the food.

"Why am I not surprised you have an apartment in your office?"

"Because I'm sure you do, too."

He turned around, still smiling. "You know I do."

Her heart lurched just a bit because she did know. They'd always joked that when they were big in the corporate world they'd need an apartment in their office because they'd never want to leave. Making money was all that had mattered to Cole back in the day, while being powerful enough to fill her father's shoes had been her main objective.

Guess they both got their wish. But as she looked back, the old saying came back to bite her in the butt... "Be careful what you wish for."

5:15. Tamera pulled her BMW into the marina and cringed. She hated being late, but today was the day from hell and there was nothing she could do about it. TGIF at least.

She glanced down at her clothes and groaned. Still wearing her running shorts, sports bra and racer-back tank, she knew Cole would wonder what on earth she'd been doing.

Tamera grabbed her purse and her sketches that they'd worked on at the office and made a mad dash down the dock toward Cole's million-dollar yacht. The palm trees overhead rustled in the breeze, mocking her. The sun beat down, making her already break into a sweat. Unfortunately, she didn't have time to appreciate the swaying palms, the pristine white boats docked here or even the sultry heat.

No, her day had been spent inside, talking with health care workers about her father and then administering to his needs. She didn't have time to focus on the simple things…not when her father's life was slowly drawing to a close and his entire empire hinged on her making this deal a success.

It was the least she could do for a legacy he'd handed down with the utmost faith in her abilities.

Tamera held her hand over her brows to block the sun as she stared ahead to Cole's yacht. He stood on the dock watching for her. The sun illuminated his broad shoulders, making him seem even more dominating, more powerful.

"I know, I'm late," Tamera said in a rush as she reached him. "I'll apologize for both that and my less-than-professional appearance."

After he assisted her on board, he climbed on himself. "Just get back from a workout?"

"I wish." She followed him down into the galley and laid her sketches on the table and her purse on the sofa. "I was leaving for my morning run when the hospice nurse called and said they needed to see me right away. Needless to say, I didn't take time to change."

"Everything okay?" Cole grabbed a bottle of water from the bar and passed it to her.

Tamera unscrewed the cap and took a cool, refreshing drink. "Nothing that we hadn't expected. His blood counts are off and his medications needed to be adjusted."

Cole leaned a hip on the edge of a barstool. "So why did they call you so early?"

"Because he had a bad night and was asking for me." Guilt crept up and nearly suffocated her. "I hate that he's in an unfamiliar place with strangers. I wasn't there when he needed me."

Cole closed the small gap between them and took her by the shoulders. "Go back to your father."

Shaking her head, she clutched the water bottle. "No, I need to do this. He was resting when I left, so he's fine. The nurses have my number and will call if they need to. I'll swing by there when I leave here anyway."

The muscle in Cole's jaw ticked. "You run yourself too thin. The nurses have everything under control. You need someone to look out for you for a change."

She brushed him aside and bent to get her sketches. "I don't have time to be spoiled or pampered, Cole. I have to work."

Besides, she thought, there was no one else to take care of her. Her father was all she had left. Oh, she had friends and business associates, but if something were to really happen to her, who would she turn to?

Cole? What would he do? He was nothing more than a business associate at this point. Right?

"If you insist on stressing yourself over this, then at least have a seat." He gestured to the small work area he'd set up with leather club chairs and a glass table. "The offer remains, though, I can work on this tonight and we can go over it sometime over the weekend if you want to leave."

"Cole, I'm fine. Can we just work?"

Obviously he was concerned about her. The way he kept staring at her as if he were waiting for her to pass out or break down and cry was disconcerting. But she'd be damned if she'd show weakness. It was bad enough that she'd fallen asleep in his arms the other night, no way could she appear to be anything less than on top of her game now.

Cole nodded. "Whenever you want to eat, I had my chef prepare some food and we can dine out on the deck."

"I'm not hungry right now. I'll let you know."

Cole booted up his laptop while Tamera spread out her sketches. As they worked in harmony, it was really hard not to recall another place and time when they'd worked without speaking a word and their ideas just melded together into one glorious plan.

They'd had such high hopes of being partners in a firm one day. Now here they were, working together, but to gain prestige in their own individual companies.

After about an hour, Tamera's cell rang, jarring her from her groove of design.

She rushed forward to her purse and pulled out her BlackBerry. "Hello."

"Mrs. Stevens? This is Camille from the hospice center."

Tamera turned back to Cole, who gestured for her to take her call in the bedroom.

"Is something wrong?" she asked, stepping into the captain's quarters, closing the door. "Is my father okay?"

"Yes, yes dear," the elderly lady assured her. "That's why I'm calling. The day nurse told me you'd been here all day. I was off last night, but I heard he had a bad evening. Anyway, I wanted to let you know that I'm pulling a long shift and I'll be here 'til morning. Right now your father is eating a bit and he seems content. I just wanted to keep your mind at ease."

Tamera sagged on the king-sized bed with relief. "Thank you, Camille. You don't know how much I appreciate all you guys are doing to keep him satisfied."

"Oh, dear, that's our job. We're here for Mr. Stevens and his family. Have a good night."

Tamera disconnected the call and rested her elbows on her knees, head and cell in her hands.

"Tamera," Cole said, coming into the room. "Everything okay?"

She looked up and nodded. "Yes. The nightshift nurse just wanted to let me know my father was doing okay and eating."

"Which is what you should be doing," he told her.

Tamera shook her head. "I don't need anything. We need to get this outline completed so we can present a flawless plan to Victor on Monday afternoon."

Cole stepped forward. "You need to rest."

"Why do you keep insisting on what I should be doing? I'm fine."

"You have circles under your eyes and you're looking pale." He squatted down before her. "Take thirty minutes and rest here. I can get the food set out and make sure everything's ready while you take a breather. No is not an option."

Tamera looked down at this man who insisted on doing for her what she should be doing for herself. Without notice or warning, tears sprang to her eyes. She laid her cell beside her on the bed and covered her face with her hands.

"Hey. Come now, Tamera." Cole grabbed her wrists and pulled her forward, looping her arms around his neck. "Don't do this to yourself."

"It's just, when my c-cell rings, I get so scared."

She hadn't even admitted that until now. But she knew the day was coming when the nurse would call and tell her that her father had passed.

"I know," he whispered. "Let me care for you. Just for a few minutes."

Tamera nodded, unable to fight any more tonight. "Only thirty minutes. Get the food ready and I'll be out."

Cole kissed her on the forehead and urged her down onto the bed. He pulled off her tennis shoes and tugged the navy throw from the end of the bed over her legs.

"I'll yell when it's all set up. Just rest."

Tamera smiled, closed her eyes, giving in to the fatigue that overwhelmed her.

Ten

One hour turned into two and Cole didn't care. He could've stood in the doorway to his master suite and watched the rise and fall of Tamera's chest for two more hours.

He wasn't denying himself the opportunity to watch her. No, this wasn't professional, but they had long since passed professionalism. They'd teetered on a fine line and damn if he wasn't less than an inch from crossing over.

Between checking on Tam while she rested, he'd tweaked the design more and had pretty much gotten it to where he and Tamera had wanted. Hopefully, that would be where Victor wanted as well.

His eyes traveled down the dip in Tam's waist and up over the swell of her hip. When he'd seen her rushing down the dock in nothing more than skimpy workout shorts and a tank, he nearly dropped to his knees and thanked God.

He'd ached to see her smooth, creamy skin once again. But, on the other hand, if he wasn't touching her, he felt cheated. There wasn't a man alive who wouldn't want to run his hands over those well-toned curves. Cole wanted nothing more than to reacquaint himself with everything Tamera had hidden beneath her vulnerable exterior.

She hadn't moved. Since the moment he'd covered her with the navy throw, she'd slept peacefully. He didn't want to wake her, not only because he knew she'd be furious that he'd let her sleep this long, but because she needed the rest. She was running herself ragged and if she didn't want to take care of herself, then he damn well would.

But he wouldn't let his heart get into this mix. No, he was strictly looking out for her because they were working on the biggest project of their careers.

Cole crossed the room, gave her shoulder a gentle shake and waited on her lids to flutter, waited to see those vibrant eyes shine with irritation. They didn't.

Damn. She was in a deep sleep which required him to do more than a subtle approach. Wonderful.

He eased onto the edge of the bed, running his finger along the satiny softness of her bare arm. Her skin instantly reacted by popping out in goose bumps. Always so responsive. That was one thing he'd remembered, and loved, about her.

"Tamera."

He didn't raise his voice. To be honest he wanted her to sleep, but he didn't want her to regret waking up in his bed in the morning. If she was going to sleep here, he wanted her to be fully aware of why she was there and what she was doing…and he wanted the benefits of having her in his bed.

"Tam."

Running his palm down her arm and back up over the curve of her shoulder, he watched as she started to come to. She rolled over onto her back, her arm went above her head, doing amazing things to the pull of her tight, white tank over her breasts.

Desire stirred even more in his gut. This woman was really testing his control. Of course, he could get up, walk away and let her wake on her own. He could, but he wouldn't.

"Wake up, Tam, before you hate me even more."

She let out a little moan, her lids slowly lifting, blinking against the subtle light filtering in through the doorway from the galley.

The awakening was just as beautiful as the rest. Her eyes focused on his face, as if she were struggling to figure out where she was. But her gaze never left his and that irritation he'd expected to see was absent. In its place…pure desire.

The silence aboard his yacht enveloped them, as did the darkened room. With just the glimpse of light, Cole could barely make out her face, but the slant of the glowing lamp from the galley made her eyes sparkle.

Instinct had Cole not thinking of his actions. He leaned down slowly, giving her ample time to resist or to stop this moment from happening. It was inevitable, though. They were meant to be here, right now. The project had nothing whatsoever to do with what was about to take place.

And he knew precisely once he started kissing her in his bed, neither of them were going to get back to work tonight.

Her eyes shifted to his mouth as her tongue darted out, moistening her plump lips. The invitation was clear, all he had to do was accept.

"Be sure," he warned, a split second before he closed the gap and captured her mouth beneath his.

The sudden intake of breath from Tamera was quickly followed by total abandonment. He knew she wouldn't fight him, not on this. Not when everything that had transpired before this moment had led them here.

This is where he'd wanted her since being reunited in that boardroom weeks ago. The familiarity of her kiss, her touch, rushed back to him and he had to clamp down those long-ago buried memories of love and foolishness and concentrate on the now. This was nothing more than physical attraction. Absolutely. Nothing. More.

Cole rested his hands on either side of her face, the feather pillow giving beneath his weight. Nothing could be sweeter than getting Tamera back in his bed.

Not only did he want her for purely selfish reasons, he wanted that instant gratification he'd receive knowing he'd won. He'd not only bettered himself to a level Tam's father never would've believed, but he also got Tamera right where he wanted her. In bed.

Love was definitely not something he wanted at this point in life. Why would anyone need love when there were contracts to be won, designs and structures to be created?

No, what he wanted was right here beneath him. Tamera's warm, willing body moving in a familiar rhythm with his. She was more than accepting, more than giving.

Her hands came up, wrapped around his neck and toyed with his hair. Subtle touches were one of the things he remembered most about Tamera. The woman was potent, but in an easy, nonaggressive way. But she made her point just the same and she continued to give as much into the kiss as he took.

Cole kept his body weight on one hand and allowed the other hand to move freely down the side of her curvy yet trim body. He wanted her out of these clothes five minutes ago, but he couldn't rush, not when he was so close to getting what he wanted.

Still in a dreamlike state, Tam arched her body beneath Cole's, silently begging him to rip her clothes off and take what they both had been denying themselves for weeks.

The weight of his body felt so familiar, so good pressing against hers. Consequences would come soon enough, as would regrets, but right now she needed, wanted, Cole to possess her. She wanted him to take control. She didn't want to think about what she was doing or where this would lead.

Nothing mattered but what she was feeling now and how much she'd missed the touch of a man. The touch of Cole.

Sensations she'd only experienced long ago tingled down through her body as Cole's hand slid behind her bare thigh, lifting her leg.

"Cole."

So much for silent begging. Her body had far surpassed the longing and craving of normal sexual desires. The need to feel his skin against hers consumed her and she didn't care if she did beg…so long as it got her closer to what she needed.

His hand moved to the elastic waistband of her running shorts. He lifted his body slightly and tugged the shorts down. Tamera scissor kicked her legs to move the unwanted garment on down the line.

Cole trailed kisses down her neck. "You feel so good," he murmured.

She could feel better if he'd finish this undressing process instead of chitchat. Obviously she was going to have to take control here for a bit. She tugged at his Polo shirt until it flew across the cabin to parts unknown.

Before he could settle back down against her, though, she placed both hands on his chiseled chest.

"Wait." Her fingertips explored every dip of smooth, hard muscle beneath bronzed skin. "Just…let me…"

Words were lost as Cole crushed her mouth beneath his, still keeping his chest levered off hers. As she continued to run her fingers over his pecs, his hips tilted into her.

Perhaps his desire *was* as urgent as hers.

Cole broke the kiss, sat up and pulled her up with him. Sitting on their knees, they made quick work discarding the rest of their clothing.

Then they froze.

Tamera's eyes traveled over Cole's as his did the same over hers. The gentle light streaming through the doorway beamed just enough glow across the bed to provide a romantic ambiance. Though romance was the last thing either of them were looking for…at least she wasn't and she highly doubted Cole was.

"Amazing," he whispered. "I didn't think you could get more stunning."

Tamera smiled. "Cole, I'm already naked, there's no need for compliments."

Fingertips trailed over her collarbone, down the slope of her bare breasts. "Perfect."

Cole's mouth dropped to her nipple as his hands

wrapped around her waist. Tamera's head dropped back as sensation after sensation of arousal coursed through her.

The force of his affection on her chest had her falling backward again. Cole followed her down, hands roaming up and down her sides as he turned his attention to the other breast.

Tamera wrapped her legs around his waist, urging him to hurry.

He lifted his head, quirked a smile and fumbled with the bedside table until he revealed a condom. Once he was ready, he glanced down to the part in her legs and guided himself in.

Tamera watched his face, hoping he'd look at her, but he kept his eyes closed. Distance. He was still keeping distance.

Perhaps she should do the same. After all, she didn't want more than tonight…did she?

No, no way could she put herself on the line any more than that where this Casanova was concerned. She would take this moment and revel in it, but then she would get back to business and hopefully get Cole out of her system and her life. Maybe she could finally have closure. Maybe.

Their bodies moved in an urgent need. Tamera locked her ankles, keeping Cole right where she wanted him.

As her climax slammed into her, Cole's body arched above hers, the muscles in his biceps straining as he held himself still.

Once the tremors ceased, Tamera waited to see what he would do, say. She didn't know what she expected, a little term of endearment, a little kissing, snuggling maybe, but him levering himself up off her and immediately getting dressed? No, that was not what she'd expected at all.

But this colder side of Cole was no match for the iciness she'd encountered years ago. She should be used to his reaction toward her. Still, she pulled the soft sheet up over her chest, suddenly feeling the chill.

"I'll be in the galley when you want to come in and finish working," he told her before disappearing into the living area.

Ahh, the romance. Not that she was looking for it, but seriously? Couldn't he have just thrown a bucket of cold water on her? The freezing effect would be just the same.

Eleven

Cole pulled a beer from the mini fridge beneath his bar and twisted the lid off. Well, he'd gotten what he'd wanted, now what? Tamera certainly wasn't out of his system. If anything, she was deeper under his skin.

How the hell had his perfect plan backfired? He'd gotten her in his bed by purposely having them meet aboard his yacht, yet her vulnerability made him feel like a complete ass for taking advantage.

God, he was even contradicting himself. Did he or did he not want to seduce her just because he still could? Did he not just get what he wanted, on his own turf? And was he not still just as frustrated as he'd been before?

To top the icing on the proverbial cake, he'd treated her like a cheap hooker when he'd all but jumped out of bed, discarded the condom and basically ordered her back to work.

Smooth, really smooth.

Good thing he wasn't looking for romance or love, because those qualities were obviously long gone.

He heard her shuffle across the carpeted galley, but didn't turn. He wasn't ready to see the regret or hurt that would no doubt be in her eyes.

She opened the larger refrigerator, moved some things around and finally closed the door. Cole moved over to the work area he'd set up on his long, rectangular table before she'd arrived.

While she'd been asleep, he'd spread out her sketches and worked off them. Now, he returned to the work he'd done mere moments ago.

Yet so much had changed since he'd stood here last time.

Tamera came around to the table. From the corner of his eye, he noted she'd dressed in her running wear again, right down to the tennis shoes. She stood sipping a bottle of water, glancing down at her designs, which he'd altered.

"You need something to eat," he told her, keeping his gaze on the table.

"I don't like what you did here." She ignored his remark and pointed to the entryway of the hotel. "This wall cuts off that airy feeling we were going for."

He followed her perfectly manicured finger across the sketch to the area of the lobby they'd set aside for the registration desk. "There's no way to avoid it. They will need a safe and counter space to work and columns can only offer so much support. Especially on the ground floor."

"I don't like it," she insisted.

"I don't think it matters what you like or don't like," he snapped, turning to look at her. "Victor makes the final judgment calls and we have to be professionals about this and realize that the wall has to remain where it is."

She jerked her body around, slamming her bottle on the table…thankfully the lid was on it.

"Professional?" Her hands went to her hips. "Don't you dare question my professionalism. How professional was that?"

She pointed toward his cabin.

"That had nothing to do with business," he told her.

Tamera let out a clipped laugh. "No, you're warmer to business associates than you were to me. You're absolutely right."

Guilt wrapped around his chest and squeezed. "We both knew going into that that we were just acting on physical attraction."

Tamera held up a hand. "Forget it. Just forget it. I don't know why I expected more from you. Obviously I didn't learn from my previous experience."

She crossed to the couch, grabbed her purse and marched up the steps onto the deck.

Cole didn't have to go topside to know she was gone. She wasn't just up there getting air. She was pissed and had every right to be.

She'd be fine once she cooled off. They had to meet with Victor in two days. This design had to be completed by then. So, whenever Tamera was done with her tantrum, he'd be waiting. If nothing else, she was a professional. She wouldn't let this project fall behind simply because of what had happened in his bedroom.

Tamera knew Cole, at least the business side of him. Even though it was Saturday, the man would be in his office. There was no need to call to confirm, she didn't want to give him a heads up so he could plot and scheme more ways to make her feel inadequate.

The only way she'd call is if the front doors to his building were locked, but even then, he'd only have minutes to come up with some way to mistreat her.

After storming off his yacht last night, she'd calmed down enough to know they had a project that needed their attention. Surely they could put hormones, their past and whatever else was crackling between them on hold for the duration of this design phase.

Once Zach took over on-site for the actual construction, which would take months, she wouldn't have to see Cole nearly as much, if at all.

Tamera pulled her BMW in front of The Marcum Agency's three-story glass structure and took a deep, calming breath. Okay, so maybe it wasn't calm, but she was trying here.

She grabbed her tote bag and locked her car. The sun was shining bright today, the glare bouncing off all that shiny glass, making Tamera even more annoyed. Even the sun shone down upon the high and mighty Cole Marcum.

One tug on the door and, praise God, it opened. She took the elevator to the top floor and marched down the hall toward his office.

She heard laughter. Female laughter.

Two-timing jerk.

Wait. Two-timing? No. That would imply that she and Cole had a relationship. They'd had sex. Big difference.

Tamera shifted her white designer bag on her shoulder, smoothed a hand down her pale yellow sheath. Taking another deep breath, she entered Cole's office where she encountered the body behind the female voice.

Kayla.

"Tamera," Cole's sister exclaimed, rushing across the room. "What are you doing here?"

Tamera accepted her old friend's hug. No matter what had transpired between her and Cole, Tamera had always held a special place in her heart for Kayla. She was most definitely the sister she'd never had…too bad they'd lost touch.

"I came to work," Tamera replied, easing back to look at Kayla. "You're still stunning."

Kayla, being a shy woman, simply smiled. "I didn't know you and Cole had a meeting set for today."

Tamera eyed the man in question, who seemed perfectly content to lean against the corner of his desk and smirk. Okay, he may not have been two-timing, but he was still a jerk.

"We didn't. We do have a meeting with Victor Lawson on Monday and we need to finalize some plans. I just assumed Cole would be in his office today."

"No rest for the weary," Zach chimed in.

Tamera turned and smiled as Cole's twin strode across the office with a folder.

"Here's the construction company I'm looking at." Zach handed the folder to Cole. "If you want to run this by Victor and see if he knows anything about them. We haven't used them before, but they do specialize in resorts all over the country, some in Mexico. I've seen their work and haven't heard one complaint or negative remark."

Cole nodded. "Thanks. You heading home?"

Zach glanced to his watch. "Probably should. I have to pick up Sasha at three."

"Sasha?" Kayla threw a questioning look at Tamera. "I've never heard of her."

"We just met."

"And no further explanation will be given," Kayla finished.

Zach laughed and pecked his sister's cheek. "Good to see you again, Tamera. I suppose I have you to thank for getting my brother in a sour mood today. It's good to see him knocked off that high horse every now and again."

Zach strode out whistling.

"I have to leave as well." Kayla went over to the boardroom-style table across the room and grabbed her purse. "I'm meeting some friends for a late lunch."

She hugged Tamera once again. "I hope we can get together for something other than business."

Tamera's heart squeezed. She knew she'd missed the female companionship of Kayla, but she hadn't realized how much. "I'd like that."

"Cole," Kayla called over her shoulder as she headed toward the door. "Call me after the meeting and let me know how it goes."

Cole nodded, still not saying a word. He really was in a mood. Oh well, if he was, it was of his own doing. He'd initiated things last night, and he was the one who'd left her behind in the bed. She'd felt just as cheap as if he'd thrown money onto the nightstand.

Tamera glanced at the boardroom table and noticed her sketches spread out, much like they had been at his yacht last night. She moved over to them, shifting the large, three-ring binders out of the way.

"I'm glad you came to your senses."

Tamera ignored Cole's jab at her work ethic. She would not start this day with him with an argument. That would do nothing but waste time and make her feel worse than she already did. And if he was in a bad mood, then by all means who was she to help him out of it? He deserved to live in a bit of misery after all he'd done to her…and not just last night.

Her eyes scanned the papers, but one particular area caught her eyes and tugged at her heart.

"You changed the registration area," she murmured, tracing her finger over the new design.

Tamera threw a glance over her shoulder as Cole moved like a predator across the room. He filled out his crisp white, button-down shirt and dark, designer jeans. Did the man have to look handsome every moment of every blasted day?

"Zach and I worked on this last night and this morning."

"Last night?"

Cole nodded, coming to stand directly beside her. "He met me here and we worked until about two and then I came back in about nine. I caught a few hours in my bed," he gestured toward the makeshift apartment.

Well, lack of sleep would certainly put a damper on anyone's mood, but Cole didn't look sleep deprived… he looked torn.

Was he regretting last night? Was he sorry they'd been intimate or was he sorry about his actions afterward? Tamera knew in her heart, that even if he was remorseful for what he'd done, he wouldn't admit it. Cole Marcum would never admit to weakness or being wrong.

Damn prideful man. Just like her father.

She drew her attention back to the drawing. "This is exactly how I wanted it."

Cole reached across the table, picked up the binder and slammed it shut. He took it and placed it back on the floor-to-ceiling shelves stacked with numerous other black binders containing designs and sample materials for the firm's projects.

"Did Zach think this was a good idea?" Tamera asked, trying to get a sense of what exactly Cole was mad about.

Cole turned, settled his hands on his hips and shrugged. "He said it would work either way."

"Then why did you remove a good portion of the wall?"

"I just did." He pulled out another sheet, this one for the top floor, and laid it over the one she'd been studying. "We need to work on the details for the ballrooms."

Okay, so that topic was closed.

Had Cole done the redesigning out of guilt because they'd had sex? Tamera felt absurd even thinking such a thing, but why else would he have worked so late into the night? And why else would he have called Zach in?

Perhaps Cole wasn't the jerk she'd deemed him to be. Perhaps he did have a heart after all.

Or perhaps he just thought he could get into her good graces again and get her back into bed.

Twelve

"**I** don't know why we need to have a meeting without Tamera," Kayla stated as she took a seat on the black leather sofa in Cole's makeshift apartment adjacent to his office.

Cole poured himself a shot of whiskey. "Because we've run into a glitch."

Zach breezed through the door. "What the hell is the big emergency? I need to finish these calls I have out to this construction company before I take off for the day."

"Have a seat." Cole motioned to the vacant cushion beside their sister.

Zach stopped in his tracks. "Oh, no. What have you done?"

Cole eased a hip onto the barstool, rested an elbow against the bar and swirled his drink. "I didn't do anything. I have something I need to run by you two."

"Why isn't Tamera here?" Kayla repeated, crossing her legs and quirking a brow.

"Have a seat, Zach." Cole eyed his brother until his twin propped himself on the arm of the sofa next to Kayla. "Walter Stevens is dying. He's in hospice care right now."

"Oh, poor Tamera." Kayla put a hand up to her mouth, tears already forming in her eyes. "How is she holding up?"

"Just like you'd expect her to," Cole confirmed. "She's stubborn, won't accept help from anyone and is insistent she can run things herself."

Zach and Kayla shared a look, like they had some private joke between them.

"What?" Cole asked.

"Sounds like you," Kayla told him. "She's not going to show her weakness, Cole. You of all people should appreciate that."

Appreciate it? The woman was damn near driving him insane with her stubbornness.

He waved with his drink. "We're getting off track here. With Walter dying, the fate of The Stevens Group hinges on Tamera and her ability to run the company as well as her father and grandfather did."

Zach shrugged. "Okay, so?"

"There's no reason we can't make her an offer." Cole set his glass on the bar and came to his feet. "Tamera is vulnerable right now and will be even more so after Walter's death. I don't see why we can't approach her about joining forces."

The look was exchanged once again between his siblings.

"Has Tamera hinted that she's uncomfortable with running the company?" Kayla asked.

"No."

"Then what makes you think this is even a good idea?" Zach piped in.

Cole paced to the windows where he looked out onto the bay. "Because…this merger would benefit our firm…if we combine forces, just think of all we could accomplish."

"This has nothing to do with what's going on between the two of you personally?" Zach questioned.

Cole glanced back to his twin, who sat with a knowing smirk. "No, this is strictly business."

He turned his attention back to the crystal blue water, lined with tall, sturdy palm trees.

"I don't think it's a good idea," Kayla said. "I think it's low to dive in and attack while she's down. And it's even worse you're planning the attack for when she'll be the lowest."

Cole shoved his hands in his pockets, turned and leaned against the warm glass. "It's not an attack, Kayla. It's a good business move for both of us."

"Says who?" Zach demanded. "The Stevens Group has been around longer than we have. Why would they suddenly merge with us?"

"Because Tamera isn't stupid. She's seen what we can accomplish and with both our names on Victor's hotel, clients will want us as a package deal in the future."

"So, you're just going to ask Tamera to sell her father's legacy, the only substantial thing she has left of him, and come to work with us?" Zach shook his head, laughed. "Yeah. That'll go over well."

"She'll think this was all her idea," Cole countered. "All I will do is encourage her. I need to know what you two think."

Kayla ran a hand down her black, glossy hair and

shoved it past her shoulders. "I think it would be a fantastic business move for us, but on a personal level, I don't think it's wise. You and Tamera share a past. Should you keep this entanglement going?"

Should he? Was he just asking for more trouble down the road? Perhaps, but in his life, business came first. No matter what.

Kayla came to her feet, smoothed her hands down her red sheath and smiled. "Cole, when you find out what Tamera really wants, then we'll talk. Until then, I think this is a premature conversation."

With her quiet, easy manner, Kayla left the room, leaving Zach behind.

"Go ahead," Cole said to his twin. "I know you want to say something."

Zach stood and crossed to the window to stand beside Cole. "Have you lost your mind?"

"Not yet."

Zach rubbed his stubbled jaw. "Who are you trying to prove something to, Cole? Tamera, her father, or yourself? Walter is dying. He doesn't care what you do anymore. This competition is completely one-sided."

Cole fisted his hands. "I'm not proving anything. I'm trying to move us into a better direction."

"I didn't know we were going in the wrong direction," Zach mocked. "If this is about your guilt over a decision you made years ago, move on."

Thankfully Zach hadn't mentioned that aspect while Kayla had been in the room. Kayla had never been told the real reason for the breakup. She would've no doubt gone and told Tamera which, in turn, would've caused a rift between Tamera and her only living family member.

"I've moved on." Cole gritted his teeth, narrowing

his gaze at his brother. "We both know this is a good move."

"Maybe it is, but at what cost?"

Zach crossed the room and left the office. Cole hated that Zach was always so easygoing, yet to the point. The man knew just how to pinpoint the heart of a problem. He was a man of few words, but when he spoke, they were important.

Zach was right, though. At what, or should he say whose, cost would this merger be carried out?

Running a hand through his hair, Cole moved from the living area back out into his office. He was already thinking in terms of this merger being a done deal. There was no way, no way Tamera would give in to this business arrangement. But she had to think reasonably. The pressure would be too great for her to run a multimillion-dollar company and deal with the grief of losing her father, when that time came.

Cole took a seat behind his desk and wiggled his mouse to bring his computer back to life. Who was he kidding? Tamera was more than capable of running— successfully he might add—Walter's company. Hadn't she done so already without anyone's knowledge as to where her father was?

The truth ate at Cole. He hated admitting it even to himself.

He wanted Tamera working with him. Period. She was intelligent, resourceful and determined. If she weren't so stunning, those qualities in themselves would have him attracted to her.

But she was stunning. Just the thought of her had him catching his breath. He could admit, only because he was alone, that he wanted her on his team so he could keep an eye on her. He wanted to know what she was doing in business and her personal life at all times. Call it overbearing, he didn't care. He didn't want to let Tamera out of his life again.

No, he didn't want love. No, he didn't want a relationship. He was simply incapable of those two things. But he wasn't immune to caring.

So, Tamera would have to see his side of things. He'd make sure of it. And, in the end, she'd come to work for The Marcum Agency thinking everything was her idea.

Thirteen

"Amazing."

Tamera crossed her legs and watched as Victor scanned through the first draft of his first American hotel. He sat across from her and Cole at the long boardroom table in Cole's office.

Trying to appear calm, Tamera resisted looking over at her co-designer sitting directly to her right.

"The exterior is absolutely perfect," he said, his eyes still riveted to the drawing. "Breathtaking."

Tamera couldn't stop the grin from spreading across her face. "We wanted to give guests a feel of another time and place. Something extravagant, classic and timeless."

He lifted his gaze, looking between her and Cole. "You two make a great team. I knew I'd made the right choice hiring both agencies. Have you ever thought of joining forces? You'd monopolize the architectural world."

Okay, that comment made her a bit squeamish. She didn't want to be a "great team" with Cole any more than she wanted to "join forces." Those days were long gone…and the other night aboard his yacht didn't count.

She'd thought that using him, just as he'd done her, would make her feel better, powerful. Quite the opposite. She felt even worse about herself and this entire pairing.

A boardroom union was fine for now, but this was not something she wanted in the long run. Her emotional state had already taken a beating and she'd only worked with Cole for a few weeks.

"We have enjoyed working on this project," Tamera piped up.

Victor glanced down to the spread of drawings. "It shows."

"Shall we go on to look at materials for the exterior?" Cole asked.

"I actually had my assistant e-mail you both as I was on my way here," Victor said. "In her message is everything I want to see as far as textures, lighting, metals, in both the exterior and interior. I have another meeting in South Beach in thirty minutes. I appreciate the use of your office seeing as how I had several places to be today and this was on my way."

"Not a problem," Cole said. "Anywhere that's convenient for you to meet is fine with us. We're here for you."

When Victor came to his feet, looking at his watch, Tamera and Cole rose as well.

"If you have any questions, please feel free to

contact me or my assistant and she can get ahold of me," he continued as he walked to the door. "Zach and I have a meeting scheduled later in the week to discuss contractors. I'm pleased with how quickly this project is moving."

"The Marcum Agency is efficient," Cole beamed.

Victor nodded. "I will be in touch."

As soon as he was out the door, Tamera resisted the urge to slam it, simply shutting it with a louder than average click.

"What the hell was that?" she demanded, whirling around on Cole.

"What?"

She clutched the door handle behind her with both hands so she wouldn't be tempted to strangle him. "You implied your agency is more efficient than mine. We are in this together as a team, which means we're equals."

"I never said otherwise." Cole turned his back on her, walked over to the table and began straightening the papers.

Tamera tried counting to ten, but only made it to three. "Don't brush me off like some child."

"Then quit acting like one," he said, still with his broad back to her.

She marched around to stand in front of him. "You are being deliberately rude and hateful."

His hands froze on the papers he was holding as he shifted to face her completely. "Am I? Perhaps you're just too sensitive because you're overworked lately. Why don't you take the rest of the day off and rest?"

Fury that had been rising to the surface for the past minute finally bubbled over. "You may be used to bossing your staff around, but I do not work for you. I work for myself and, at the moment, Victor. And I don't have time to rest, not with all that is going on."

The muscle in Cole's jaw ticked. "You've been to see your father today?"

"Yes."

"Going back?"

Tamera shook her head. "I will probably go after dinner and see that he's settled in for the night."

"When are you going to tell people about him? They're going to find out soon enough."

Tamera didn't want to think about what would happen "soon enough." "I'm not worried about that right now, Cole. Hospice is caring for him."

"Is he at Mercy Hospice Center?"

"Yes."

Cole brushed the pads of his thumbs beneath her eyes, his hands came to rest on her shoulders. "You're not taking care of yourself."

Uneasy with the fact he knew her so well, Tamera took a step back, forcing Cole's hands away. "I don't have a choice. You know that."

"If you're not going to relax, at least do something for just you that isn't work."

Tam laughed. "Yeah. When would I have time for that?"

He studied her face, his eyes lingering on her lips a bit longer than she was comfortable with. "Let's celebrate tonight after you go see your father."

She jerked back, stunned. "Celebrate? What?"

"Victor's stamp of approval." Cole moved closer. "We need to concentrate on nothing but having a good time. It'll do wonders for you."

Tamera thought of the possibilities that could come from spending an evening with Cole "having a good time." She deserved as much, though, didn't she? She could more than handle his charms and she'd throw a few of her own his way if he got out of hand.

What could going out hurt? She'd have her cell if the nurses needed to get ahold of her. A night without cares was exactly what she needed.

"Maybe." She smiled, already looking forward to the endless possibilities. "Where do you want to go?"

"We'll stay in South Beach. Find a nice club, some dinner."

Tamera nodded, wondering exactly what his motives were. Cole didn't do anything, she'd noticed, without gaining something to his benefit.

"Fine."

Cole gestured toward the designs and the piles of black binders. "When do you want to meet again to work on the final draft and intricate details before passing them on to Zach?"

Tamera's week of events rolled through her head. "I probably can't do anything until Friday. I have late meetings and I have dinner with Dad two nights."

"Do you want to come here or do you want to meet somewhere after work?"

Memories of him waking her, his hands undressing her, his mouth on her body consumed her. "I think it's best we meet in the office. Mine."

A cocky smirk tilted the corner of his mouth. "If I want you, Tamera, the location won't matter."

"You bastard," she whispered. "If you think you can have me on a whim and discard me whenever you feel like it, you're insane. I may have been foolish once the other night, but it won't happen again."

Cole snatched her around her waist and tugged her flush with his body at the same time his mouth came down on hers. She struggled for about two seconds before kissing him back.

If nothing else, the man knew how to kiss.

She didn't give him the satisfaction of touching him back, though. She kept her hands dangling at her sides. No, she was taking this kiss and giving nothing back.

His lips were rough, demanding and Tamera's body betrayed her by letting out a soft moan.

Cole pulled back. "Don't lie to me or to yourself. It will happen again."

The heat in his eyes combined with his promissory tone had Tamera pulling from his hold, grabbing her purse and all but running from the room.

"Pick you up at eight," he yelled just before she slammed the door.

Cole cursed himself for allowing Tamera to get the best of him, making him lose his control. He wasn't lying, though, when he told her he could have her whenever he wanted. He wasn't oblivious to the fact she melted every time he touched her. She was not lost to the fact they were still attracted to each other.

"Everything okay?"

Cole turned from the conference table to see Zach standing in his doorway. "Fine."

"Then why do you look like you just ate a sack of nails?"

Cole did not want to deal with his twin right now. "Busy here, Zach. What do you need?"

His brother crossed the room to the long table and picked up a sheet of paper, studied it. "First, let's start with why Tamera stormed out of here, nearly knocking me over in the hallway, then acting as if she didn't even see me."

Cole snatched the sketch from Zach's hand. "Ask her."

"I'm asking you," he said, leaning against the table, crossing his arms over his chest. "You didn't mention the notion of her coming to work here, did you?"

"No. She's got a lot on her plate right now, that's all." Cole wasn't about to elaborate further, not even with his twin. "We're going out tonight to celebrate. She'll be fine."

He'd make sure of it. Because at the end of the night, she was going to be back in his bed. And, unlike last time, she'd be more than satisfied with his performance afterward.

"Going out?" Zach asked. "I thought you weren't going to get entangled with her again. And don't tell me this is another business meeting."

"Not business. I don't plan on doing any business tonight."

Zach let out a low whistle. "Doesn't sound like you're trying to avoid the entanglement, Cole. Sounds like you're weaving the web."

Cole shrugged. "Perhaps I am, but I'm still in control of where I lay the threads."

"Just get this design done, make Victor happy and let me step in and do what I do best. Build. And don't screw with Tamera's head again. She's in a fragile state right now. You of all people should understand that."

Cole gave a mock salute. "If you're done harassing me, I need to get back to work so I can get ready for my evening."

"Don't screw this up."

Zach walked out, closing the door behind him.

Screw this up? What exactly was he referring to?

Didn't matter, really. Cole didn't intend on screwing

anything up. Not the agreement they had going with Victor Lawson and certainly not this evening he had planned with Tamera.

He intended to take Tamera to the hottest nightclub and dance so close to her, she'd be begging him to take her home. He wanted to feel her body close to his again. He wanted to make her blue eyes go icy with desire.

But most of all, he wanted her to know he was much better now than he'd been years ago.

A curl of excitement swirled deep in her belly. Cole knew her inside and out. He knew when she needed a break, knew how hard to push to make her cave.

She didn't want to give, didn't want to acknowledge that he had so much power over her personal life.

But there you have it. Cole Marcum still held a piece of her. Sometimes she just wished it wasn't the piece that controlled her heart.

Tamera hit the button to drop the top of her sporty car. She wanted to feel a bit reckless, a bit of freedom if only for a few minutes.

The air whipped her hair around. Tam smiled as she glanced up to the clear blue sky stamped with the amazingly tall green palms lining the highway.

For once in her life she was going to forget her troubles, enjoy this opportunity fate had handed her.

If Cole was determined to show her a good time, she'd show him just exactly what she was made of.

Fourteen

Did someone order sexy?

Tamera turned from side to side, checking herself out in the floor-length mirror. Her short, red halter dress showed off her curves. The loose curls she'd put at the ends of her blond hair were bouncy, perfect for dancing. She applied a subtle gloss to make her lips appear even fuller, luscious.

If Cole wanted a hot night, he would be one extremely happy man when he knocked on her door. She wasn't letting him forget, even for a minute, what he'd let go of so long ago. Was it so wrong to rub it in every chance she got?

Why did she have to find Cole's cocky, take-charge attitude irresistible?

And even though she was still infuriated with him for those actions earlier in his office, not to mention the way he always told her how to live her life as if he knew what she was going through, she was looking forward to having a night of fun. Cole had always been a good time and she had no doubt tonight would be no exception.

Besides, she needed something positive in her life. For an hour, maybe two, she wanted to pretend her world wasn't crumbling, her emotional state wasn't so fragile.

She couldn't remember when she'd last had a night out. Not only that, she couldn't recall when she'd actually been on a date.

Date?

Tamera groaned, turning from the mirror to grab her small, silver handbag, dropping her lip gloss into the pouch.

This was most certainly *not* a date. Just because they were going out to dance, eat, and possibly end up in bed…okay, that was more probable than possible. None of that meant this was a date.

They were simply celebrating a milestone in both of their careers. Besides, Cole was right. She did need to relax, take a few moments for herself and have a good time.

So why did she feel guilty for needing this reprieve while her father lay in a hospice center living out his last days?

She jerked when her doorbell chimed. She smoothed a hand down her dress as she rushed to the door.

Cole's eyes widened as he raked his gaze over her.

Tamera was more than pleased with Cole's reaction. The flirty, saucy dress was certainly not her normal, everyday wear, but she'd been waiting for the perfect opportunity to wear it. Showing Cole what he'd missed out on was the best occasion she could think of.

But, the surprise was on her, too, when she slid her eyes down his body.

Cole wore faded jeans paired with a black T-shirt that made him look like the devil she knew him to be.

She swallowed, stepped out onto her porch and closed the door behind her.

The visual lick he gave her body from her head to her French-manicured toes made her shiver. "I'm ready."

"Yes, you are."

"Where are we going?" she asked, trying to avoid the way her body reacted to this delectable, yet infuriating man.

"Just a little club owned by a friend of mine. Great food, even better dance floor and live band."

Tamera offered a smile. "Can't wait."

He closed the gap between them, his eyes settling on the plunging V of her dress. "We'd better get going before I change my mind and we stay in to celebrate."

Yes, they'd better go because the way he kept those heavy-lidded eyes roaming over her only made her want to give in. Even though their last bedroom encounter left her feeling cold, lonely, she was feeling anything but chilly right now.

Could her feelings for this man be more all over the spectrum? One minute she wanted to throttle him, the next she wanted to strip him.

He escorted her to his sleek, black sports car that probably cost what was for some people a full year's salary. Just how many vehicles did he have? Everything about this man demanded attention and attention was precisely what she wanted to give him tonight.

Though they drove in silence, the sexual tension bouncing around in the car was deafening. In a way, she wished he'd have said to hell with it and had his way with her in her foyer.

But he knew what he was doing…and so did she. He wanted her, she wanted him. They were playing a game centuries old and in the end, they'd both win.

Cole pulled his car into a parking spot behind one of the many clubs South Beach had to offer.

"You're friends with the man who owns Live?" Impressed, Tamera glanced to see Cole's reaction.

"Zach and I redesigned the interior when Matt bought this place."

"Only certain people can get in." She couldn't believe Cole's social status. "I've always heard this place rivals the line and security Studio 54 had."

She stared at the "Live" sign hanging above the back entrance, still in awe that Cole had such connections. How many times had he used this ace in the hole to lure women back to his bed? No, she wouldn't think like that because tonight, she was the woman with him and that's all that mattered. Tonight.

"We'll get in," he assured her as he exited the car.

Cole led Tamera to the back door, his hand on the small of her back. The intimate gesture sent shivers racing through her body even on this humid evening.

With the way her dress scooped in the back, his thumb kept caressing her bare skin. Tamera didn't know if he was doing it on purpose or if it was an innocent gesture while he chatted with the security guard. Either way, the circular motion he made completely wiped her mind free. She had no idea what the two men were discussing, didn't care. Nor did she care about going into such a reputable club.

She wanted to go back home. With Cole. Now.

"Thanks, Enrique."

Tamera offered the Cuban guard a wide smile and stepped into the club when he opened the door to allow them to pass through.

Okay, she could do the club scene for a while, but then she was demanding Cole take her back home. Why was she fighting her most basic of urges?

"So you do know the secret handshake," Tamera joked as the door was closed behind them. "I should've paid attention."

Cole leaned down to her ear. "If you're nice, I'll teach you sometime."

Mercy. The man was good.

The darkened atmosphere, only illuminated by cobalt blue lights suspended from various parts of the ceiling, made this evening more intimate…as if they needed more of that.

The architect in her was impressed as she took in the two sets of wrought-iron stairs on either side of the spacious room. A stage at the far end to her left supported the amazing band belting out some sexy salsa music.

The bar was hopping with people ordering drinks. She appreciated the fact there were no chairs. She always hated maneuvering her way between bar stools to order.

Large, leather couches were dotted around the end to her right. Oversized, low ottomans were also spread about. Nearly every spot was occupied with beautiful people enjoying the renowned South Beach night life.

She turned to Cole. "Thanks for bringing me here."

His dark eyes roamed over her face, while the tip of his finger ran along her jawline. "My pleasure."

O-kay. She needed to keep the upper hand here. Yes, she wanted to relax and have a good time with Cole, but seriously. If she didn't get her emotions under a tight grasp, she'd likely find herself in the very spot she'd been in eleven years ago. And the fact that she wanted him so desperately on a physical level wasn't helping.

"I'll get you a drink," he said, moving toward the bar. "Cosmo?"

Tamera shook her head. She wanted something stronger than a drink. She wanted Cole. She wanted his hands on her, she wanted to feel his body against hers. She wanted that heat she could only get from him…no matter the chill afterward.

"No. Let's dance."

She took his hand, leading him to the crowded dance floor as the band changed their song to something even faster with a frenzied drumbeat.

Now this was what she needed. So long as she stayed in the moment, didn't let her heart get swept away by Cole's charming words, she'd be just fine. Just fine.

Tamera put her arms in the air, tossing her head from side to side as the beat of the music took over. Cole's hands circled her waist as his own hips moved to the beat.

Her flowy skirt tapped against her thighs. Her nipples puckered behind the thin material of her dress. And Cole's eyes may as well be his hands the way he kept looking over her face, her chest. The warmth and strength from his hands permeated through her silky dress.

Yeah. They wouldn't be at this club for very long. Not with the sexual tension mounting second after agonizing second. Add in the sexy atmosphere to their already growing arousal and they had the makings for some major combustion once they got alone. If they made it that long.

Tamera didn't know how long they danced. She stopped counting after three songs. All she knew was the music was awesome, the club was packed and Cole never took his eyes off her. Not once. And for a second, she found herself back in time to a place when nothing mattered but her and Cole. Their level of intimacy, their bond. Their love.

Her mouth went dry. "I'll take that drink now."

With his signature cocky grin, he nodded. Keeping one hand around her waist, Cole led her toward the bar where he ordered a foreign beer and her cosmo.

"Cole."

Tamera turned to the man who'd just come up and slapped Cole on the shoulder.

"Matt." Cole smiled and the two men did the typical male "half hug." "Good to see you," he shouted over the band.

Matt glanced at Tamera. "So you finally brought a lady into my club. About time."

What did that mean? Cole hadn't brought his dates here before? Interesting. Of course, that didn't mean a thing. Perhaps Matt just hadn't seen the women. Tamera couldn't imagine Cole *not* flaunting his abilities to get into this club, through the back door no less.

"This is Tamera Stevens," Cole introduced. "She's an associate."

Tamera reached for her drink on the bar and smiled. "Nice to meet you."

Associate? Even more interesting. Seriously, though, what did she expect him to say? This is the woman I've put through hell, slept with once recently, fought over designs with and will probably hook up with again tonight?

Yeah. Associate was much simpler.

"The pleasure is mine," Matt said, smiling at Cole. "Come on up to the VIP room and have dinner on the house."

Cole glanced at Tamera, the heat in his eyes no less than when they'd been torso to torso on the dance floor. Had someone opened the door and let the Miami heat in? Good Lord, she was sweating.

"We're going to finish our drinks and go."

Matt laughed. The man wasn't stupid. He knew exactly why they were in a hurry.

"I don't blame you," the club owner said, still smiling. "It's an open-ended invitation."

Tamera turned her attention toward the band as Matt walked away. She didn't want to appear anxious, or worse, desperate, but she was ready to yank the tie at her neck and get the night moving in an even better direction.

Cole slid the icy tip of his beer bottle across the slope of her shoulders. "Finish your drink," he bent to whisper in her ear. "We're leaving."

Say no more. Tamera took a few more swallows, knowing the swift intake settling in her empty stomach was not a good combination, especially when she needed to keep some sort of control.

She turned, set her empty glass on the bar and looked up to Cole. "Why the hurry?"

Her sweet tone, combined with a sultry smile she offered had him slamming his longneck onto the metal bar, grabbing her arm and escorting her back to the rear entrance.

Laughter bubbled deep inside her, but she didn't let it out. She'd never seen Cole lose control and if she played her cards right, she'd see it again before the night was through.

When the security guard bid them a good night, Cole merely raised his arm in a silent farewell.

Speechless as well? My, my. This was turning into an even better night than she'd planned.

Fifteen

Cole maneuvered his car, faster than usual, through the streets of South Beach toward Star Island. Tamera may think she had control over tonight, but he was going to his own turf.

He'd never taken a woman to his house. Oh, he'd taken them to his vacation homes, but never his private domain. Ever. Star Island was for invited guests only... or, it was supposed to be. And Tamera was definitely invited.

Damn this woman for getting under his skin. He didn't want this, nor did he have time for anything beyond a sexual interlude.

But he would grant Tamera the full night. They both deserved long hours of intimacy.

He pulled up to the guard, waved and drove over the bridge.

Cole looked over at Tamera. She was all but spilling

from the top of her dress. One jerk of that bow around her neck and his night of fantasies could begin.

This time of the evening was always beautiful with the magnificent homes lining the beach, their lights bouncing off the water. This was what he'd always wanted. The money, the prestige. The woman beside him.

And though his goals weren't that of a twenty-two-year-old boy, they weren't too far off. But he wasn't naïve like he was in the past. He knew whatever was going on between Tamera and him now, would likely end when their association with Victor Lawson came to a close.

But he'd conquered what he'd set out to do. Tamera was willingly coming to his home with the full intention of staying. He didn't believe she was delusional enough to think they would have anything beyond the bedroom. She was an adult and she fully knew where he stood on relationships.

Which just made this night all the more sweet. No misconceptions about what tomorrow would bring or what the next step should be. There was no next step.

The second he pulled into his circular drive he killed the engine. He'd called earlier, before he picked Tamera up, and sent his staff home with a full day's pay. He wanted this night to be completely about him and Tamera.

She was out of the car before he could round the hood and open her door. The way the bright, full moon and the exterior lights from his house lit up the driveway, she looked like an angel with all her glowing blond hair and sun-kissed skin.

Of course, he didn't think angels wore red dresses. Sexy, short, cleavage-enhancing red dresses.

Control snapped. Cole grabbed her shoulders, pushed her back against the car as his mouth descended to hers. The breasts she'd been torturing him with all evening pressed firmly against his T-shirt, making him want to rip both articles of clothing off right here in his driveway. Thank God for the privacy gates surrounding his property.

She wrapped her arms around his neck, rose on her toes to meet him and gave him everything he was demanding and more.

She eased back just enough to whisper, "Touch me."

As her mouth sought his once more, he swept her hair aside, yanked the tie around her neck and tugged on the top of the dress until she was bare and all but trembling in his arms.

"We need to get inside."

Cole picked her up, thankful she'd wrapped her legs around his waist. She buried her face in the crook of his neck and nibbled her way up to his jaw.

"You're killing me, Tam."

Once they were inside, Cole made quick work of resetting the alarm system, and sat her down on the base of the steps.

The glow from the chandelier suspended from the second floor illuminated them. The two scraps that had covered her chest all night now dangled haphazardly down her thighs.

"You'd better do more than look," she threatened with a genuine smile.

"Oh, I plan to."

He tugged his shirt from his waistband and over his head, tossing it without a sound onto the checkered, tiled floor. He stepped up onto the step below hers at the same time she kicked off her stilettos. They fell down the two stairs with a clunk.

"Condom?" she asked, her bright blue eyes heavy with passion.

He pulled one from his pocket, laid it on the newel post. "No more talking."

Once again their mouths fused as one as he lowered her to the steps.

They weren't even going to make it upstairs and that was just fine with him. Why waste time when she was feeling the urgency just as much as he was?

Cole came to his feet, leaving Tamera heaving, lying back against the stairs. He made quick work unfastening his belt, unfastening and unzipping his jeans and discarding them, along with his boxer briefs, in a puddle at his feet. He kicked aside the unwanted clothing and knelt back down, but not before reaching for the condom.

Tamera gave his body a hungry glance, then grabbed his shoulders, pulled him toward her and proceeded to make some demands of her own with that talented mouth.

Without breaking contact, Cole opened the foil packet, covered himself. He eased to the side, so he sat on the wide step and urged Tamera to straddle him.

Hands roamed in a frantic motion as he bunched the dress up at her waist and pulled on the thin scrap of panties until he had total access to what he wanted.

Without a second thought of easing into this, Cole took her. He couldn't be gentle if he tried. He'd left his control back at her house hours ago and he'd been hanging on by a mere thread since.

A quick thought flashed through his mind as to whether or not he was too rough, too demanding, but

Tamera's soft moan was all he needed to continue. She broke the kiss, rested her forehead against his and closed her eyes.

Cole wanted to watch her, though. Now that she wasn't looking, wasn't thinking, he wanted to watch her face as she lost utter and complete control. He wanted to see that moment when she didn't hold back, didn't try to be strong or put up a front. He wanted to see total abandonment.

It didn't take long.

She bit her lip, squeezed her eyes and gripped his shoulders.

So much for holding his own control. He lost his just as Tam did and closed his own eyes in an attempt to hold this feeling, this time, right where it was. To rein in all the emotion they'd formed together. Why, he couldn't say, but he wanted it just the same. How could he not? Everything about this night had been perfect. As if their past didn't exist and they were just two people who found just how compatible they truly were.

He wanted to hold this moment forever. To revel in the bliss and simplicity.

Unfortunately, that was impossible. The moment had ended all too soon. The quiet settled around them, encompassing them in its embrace. Tamera would probably want to leave, want to put him back in that professional pocket she liked to keep him in.

But he had her here all night. She couldn't go anywhere and Cole would make damn sure she'd stay until he was ready to take her home.

But he had to be careful. Anything beyond the bedroom was impossible. They'd traveled that journey before and only ended up with broken hearts.

Cole pushed past thoughts and journeys aside. He had Tamera now and now is what he'd concentrate on.

Once the tremors ceased, Cole kissed her thoroughly, slowly. He picked her up again, carried her up the wide, curved staircase toward his master bath.

His walk-in shower with six shower heads was beckoning them. And he found himself wanting to care for her, wanting to show her how she should be treated, pampered.

"You were right," she murmured in a dreamy voice, her breath warm against his neck. "I needed this."

Cole swallowed. Hard. He didn't want that warm feeling that coursed through him. He didn't want to care for Tamera any further than right now. Sex was what they had, all they could have. And it was great, so why mess with anything else?

No, he shouldn't care. But he did.

He cared what she would have to deal with in the morning, the next day and the day after that with her father and the company. He especially cared about how she was feeling about him, about this path they'd started down. He knew, in reality, there was no turning back.

He'd be lying to himself if he even tried to act like he hadn't developed new feelings for her. The problem was, what did he do with an emotion he didn't want, and had thought died long ago?

The water sluiced over them, making Cole ultra aware of just how perfect her body was. But there was so much more to Tamera than her sexy curves and beautiful nature. She was career driven, she was giving, she was everything he'd ever want in a woman…provided he was looking for one.

Yes, if he were wanting to marry and settle down, he would be a fool not to pick Tamera. Perhaps he was a fool for not choosing her now, but he just didn't have long-term abilities in him anymore.

As his hands glided over her wet skin, backing her against the tiled wall, he knew all he could offer and take in return was exactly this. And the emptiness that he knew would follow after their lovemaking would just have to be his life companion.

He had no other choice.

"Why am I not surprised you live on Star Island?"

Tamera settled deeper into the crook of Cole's arm, content for now.

"Never came up."

With the second-story patio doors open, Tamera enjoyed the moonlight and the sounds of the water rushing to shore and swaying palm trees. She appreciated the romantic ambience. Cole had provided the perfect setting, the perfect night. She wasn't surprised that the weather gods were in Cole's back pocket. Everyone else was. And she was no exception. She didn't want to get hurt again, but she had a sickening feeling that heartache and pain were inevitable where this man was concerned. All she could do was enjoy what he was offering her now.

"You always told me you'd have the best," she recalled, thinking of the dreams they'd shared with each other so long ago. "You do."

"Yes."

O-kay. Not a man of many words.

Tamera eased up onto her elbow and looked down at Cole. "Care to tell me what's wrong?"

He continued to look up to the ceiling. "Not a thing. Just thinking."

"About..."

At her prompting, he turned his gaze to her. "The past. Interesting how some things come back around."

She studied his expression, his serious tone. "You're referring to us?"

"We both know there can't be an 'us', Tamera. There can't be more to this, than, well…this."

She nodded. Though she'd told herself the very same thing, she didn't so much like hearing it come from his mouth. She'd hoped to avoid that slap in the face from reality for as long as possible.

"If you're worried I'll get caught up in the magical world of love once again, don't be." Tamera got out of bed, suddenly chilly as she went in search of…her dress, which was in the bathroom. "I have too much on my plate as well."

She moved into the spacious, tiled bathroom where she found the scrap of red right next to the massive walk-in shower. After sliding into the dress, she recalled her shoes were downstairs. And her car was not here.

This was why she always wanted her car. She hated being stranded. Especially in an awkward position. Had she been thinking beyond the "fun-filled" night he'd promised, she should've known the awkwardness would settle in.

"You're staying," Cole told her as she came back into the bedroom.

"No. I need to get back."

He pushed himself up onto his elbow. "For what?"

She sighed. "My father. I need to be available when they call."

"They have your cell. No need to rush out of here when we can enjoy the rest of our night."

He did have a point, though she wasn't sure anymore if she actually could just enjoy him. Or would she find herself wanting even more than he was willing to offer?

True, she didn't want to turn back the clock to pick up where they left off. They were too different now. But she almost wouldn't mind seeing what would happen if they started over.

Was that even possible? Had she really forgiven him for all the hurt he'd caused her? God, in eleven years if she couldn't let go of a grudge, she shouldn't be here.

Tamera stared at the gloriously naked chest, tanned and partially hidden beneath the stark white sheets. Inky hair, heavy-lidded eyes. And she knew his solid, muscular body would still be warm and welcoming.

Her dress slid back to the ground in a whoosh. He was right. Why not enjoy right now?

She had every intention of doing just that.

Cole stood in his bedroom, staring at the rumpled sheets. Images of Tamera sprawled across them, her silky blond hair spread over the satin, plagued his mind.

He'd driven her back home just an hour ago, but he missed her already. The emptiness in his twenty-thousand-square-foot home was never so prominent, so deafening.

He hadn't expected any more surprises from her, but she certainly had caught him off guard when she'd appeared like a fantasy for their date. He thought for sure she'd still be smoldering hot about that kiss in his office and how he'd called her on basically being a liar where her feelings were concerned.

But she'd taken his insults and turned them into revenge. He'd have suffered more had she not come back to his house last night. Or maybe he was suffering because of her visit.

All he knew, as he walked into the bathroom where more images of her filled his mind from when they'd showered, was that she'd broken through. She'd gotten past that wall of defenses he'd been so careful to construct.

Resting his palms against the granite counter, he leaned in toward the mirror and laughed. Ironic how an architect of his stature could build multimillion-dollar buildings and homes, yet he couldn't keep a petite woman from busting through the ironclad fort he'd built around his heart.

He ran some cool water and splashed his face, trying to make sense of where his thoughts were headed. He wasn't sure if this thing with him and Tamera would go into anything long-term. The thought petrified him, but he had to pave the way just in case.

She deserved to be treated better than the last go-round they had at a relationship. As did he.

There was only one thing to do. A step he'd known all along he needed to take.

A step that was long overdue and the clock was ticking. If he didn't act now, he would never get another chance to speak his peace and draw closure to his past.

Only then could he move forward and see what path he and Tamera would take…together.

The gleaming white tiles of the Mercy Hospice Center were nearly blinding as Cole made his way from the nurses' station toward Walter Stevens' room. He nearly chuckled at the lie he'd told the nurse to get into the room. Pretending to be the son-in-law was laughable.

He knew there wasn't much time left and Cole had something pressing to see to before the old man left this earth. More than likely nothing would come of this talk, but Cole had to stand up for the man he used to be, the man he'd become. He couldn't let his past get the better of him. And he'd regret *not* talking to Tamera's father if he didn't do it now.

He found the room at the end of the hall. The door was closed, but the nurse assured Cole that Mr. Stevens was indeed awake and, like Tamera said, having a good day…whatever that meant to a dying man.

Cole tapped on the door as he slowly opened it. He didn't know what to expect, hadn't really given it a thought, but he certainly was taken aback when a frail, balding Walter Stevens sat in the far corner in a plush rocking chair staring out the window toward the lush gardens.

The door made a slight creak and Walter turned. Cole stepped over the threshold, ready for whatever may come his way.

"What the hell are you doing here?" the old man grumbled.

The room smelled of potpourri, something fruity that no doubt Tamera had set out. Touches of her were everywhere—from the family photos on the small, white dresser to the fresh flowers beside his bed.

"I came for a talk that is eleven years overdue."

Cole crossed the room and came to stand beside the chair, but kept facing Tamera's father. The man had definitely not aged well, but chemo would probably do that to you. His skin was gray and wrinkled, his eyes a bit more sunken in than when Cole had seen him last.

"Never thought I'd see you again," Walter said, looking up to Cole. "Never really wanted to."

"Feeling's mutual," Cole replied, moving to rest against the windowsill, partially blocking the other man's view. "I'm here about Tam."

"I assumed as much." The other's man's eyes narrowed. "What about her?"

"As you know, we're working together on the Victor Lawson project." Cole took such satisfaction in seeing the man utterly speechless. "She didn't tell you? Just as well. You probably would've tried to destroy that working relationship as well."

"She wouldn't work with someone like you," Walter spouted off. "Not only is my company more prestigious in this industry, you broke her heart years ago and she's never forgiven you. I don't believe Victor Lawson would hire two companies, either. So tell me what you really want before I have you thrown out."

Cole steeled himself at the frailness of the man, but dammit, he needed to get this off his chest. He hadn't been able to confront Walter years ago, but he'd certainly do it while he had the chance.

"Ask her if you don't believe me." Cole came to his full height. "Our working relationship is beside the point, though. What you destroyed and tore apart years ago didn't break me. The only person you hurt was Tamera. I just wanted you to take satisfaction in knowing you did nothing but damage your daughter's heart and make me a stronger man. When you're long gone, my agency will far surpass yours because you were too busy trying to run Tamera's life to actually help her build a career and be happy. I also plan on having her work for me. Your company will flounder and fall."

Walter coughed and pointed up to Cole. "You listen to me. You may be wearing a thousand dollar suit, but beneath that tailor-made exterior is a punk who was and never will be suitable for my daughter. She will have no problem running my company."

Cole couldn't resist. The words just came out before he could think twice.

"No, she won't have a problem, because when we marry, the companies will merge. You may have sabotaged our past, but you won't touch our future. You have no way to blackmail me now out of her life. And if you try, you'll only hurt her in the end."

The sharp intake of breath didn't come from Tamera's father, but from the doorway. Both Cole and Walter glanced in that direction to see Tamera, white as a ghost, standing there with one hand over her mouth, the other holding on to the doorframe as if for support.

Cole didn't apologize, he'd be lying if he did, but he did cross the room to Tamera. "I'll let you two talk."

He left the room, letting Tamera and her father rehash the past he still wanted to get away from. No matter what he'd told Walter, Cole had been devastated years ago. Tamera certainly wasn't the only one hurt, but no way in hell would he ever let the old man know how much his actions destroyed Cole.

Cole only wished he'd been able to spare Tamera the pain of hearing the truth. What good would it do now? They weren't going to be in a relationship, they could barely be in the same room without arguing, unless they were having sex, but still, that didn't mean he wanted her to hurt any more than he already had.

Cole exited the building and paused in the late-afternoon sun. Obviously Tamera changed her routine and decided to not wait until after dinner to visit her father. Fate had a funny way of making things happen as they should.

Tamera was strong. If she survived their breakup years ago, she could survive the truth now.

Sixteen

"Is it true?"

Tamera forced herself to move forward and cross the room to her father. She'd decided it was such a pretty day, she'd skip work and come to get him to take him for a ride.

"Yes."

Her heart shattered all over again. How many times would she have to mend it? Would she get to a point where she just left the pieces on the floor and give up? Because even when she put it back together, there were still shards left behind that couldn't be mended.

"How could you?" She sat on the edge of the bed, unable to make her weak legs carry her any farther. "How could you purposely destroy my relationship with the one man I intended to spend the rest of my life with?"

Her father turned toward her. "I was looking out for

your future. I didn't want you to be with someone that was beneath you."

"Beneath me?" Appalled, Tamera waved a hand at him. "Nobody is beneath me. I loved him, Dad. You saw me after he broke up with me. You watched me cry every night for over a year and you still sat by and did nothing."

His eyes misted. "I'm not saying I made a mistake, but I did what I thought was right at the time."

Tamera clutched her purse in her lap. "Shouldn't I have been the one to decide what was right for my life?"

Silence. At least he wasn't going to keep defending himself. The man was stubborn and proud, so Tamera knew he wasn't going to apologize or continue to make excuses.

"So the two of you are working together?"

Tamera nodded. "I wasn't going to tell you. I didn't want you to think I was incapable of doing a project on my own."

"I would've never thought that, but I am curious as to why you didn't tell me about the Lawson project." Her father studied her beneath his sparse brows and hollowed eyes. "I knew you were bidding on it, but that was months ago, so when you didn't say anything, I assumed we didn't get it."

Aside from the fact she'd been blindsided by Cole on the day of the contract approval from Victor, Tamera had also been knocked down from celebrating when she'd come home to discover her father was only getting worse and would need round-the-clock medical care.

Added to all of that, she wanted him to be proud of her and how could he be when she hadn't even landed the project without having to team up with Cole?

"We did," she told him. "Victor has approved the preliminary plans and the final design is being drafted. Cole and I are starting to look at the various building materials to present at our next meeting with Victor."

Her father swallowed. "I'm so proud of you. I know this company is in good hands, so long as Cole Marcum keeps his off what's mine."

Tamera rubbed her forehead to clear the jumbled thoughts bouncing around. So many questions were fighting to come out of her mouth first.

"Why did you betray me?"

"I helped you," he countered. "Did you really want to spend your life with a man who couldn't even provide for his own family?"

"He was twenty years old, Dad," Tamera cried. "He'd done everything he knew to do with no parents and a grandmother who was well into her seventies."

"I wanted a man to take care of my daughter," he argued.

"I don't need to be taken care of," she shouted back. "I needed love and Cole provided that."

And that's what really hurt. He had loved her and now…who knows what he thought of her. Did it really matter at this point? He'd betrayed her just as much as her father. He could've come to her, talked to her. But he didn't.

Okay, so that's the part that hurt the most.

Oh, it all hurt, who was she kidding? Was she really debating herself over what aspect of this entire decade-long nightmare caused the most damage?

But Tamera looked back at her father and knew that their time was limited. His body was shutting down, the nurses told her that's what the yellow around his eyes and the tint to his skin meant. His liver was running on empty.

She couldn't leave this room knowing it could be for the last time and not have peace with the man who'd raised her and cared for her, though his intentions obviously weren't always the best. He was human. He made mistakes and there wasn't enough time left to argue or place blame. What was done was done.

"I forgive you." With a heavy heart, she crossed the room and kissed his forehead. "I love you, Dad."

His wrinkled hand came up to pat the arm she'd draped around his shoulders. "I didn't want you hurt. In the long run I knew it was for the best."

Perhaps he was right. Because if Cole *did* want to be with her all those years ago, he would've been. He would've found a way to fight for what he wanted.

But he hadn't.

Cole assumed Tamera would come to confront him. He was ready to defend his past actions, but he wouldn't apologize. Because he'd anticipated this, he'd told the guard to extend an open invitation to Tamera.

As she got out of her sporty BMW, Cole held the door open to his Star Island mansion. Her heeled sandals clicked on the drive as she marched with precision toward him. So much had changed since she'd been here two nights ago.

Without a word, she brushed past him and into his home as if she'd done so hundreds of times before.

Okay, so she was understandably pissed. Anger he could deal with. Hurt, not so much.

He stepped over the threshold and closed the door. Tamera had already walked through the open foyer and into his sunken living room. She stood with her back ramrod straight as she stared out the floor-to-ceiling windows overlooking the aqua bay.

"I don't know that I've ever loved and hated someone before," she said, without turning. "I didn't even know the two emotions directed at one person were possible."

Cole came to stand in front of her. If they were going to argue, they were going to do it face to face.

But he didn't see anger, or even hurt. All he saw was regret and exhaustion. Great. How could he confront her when she was clearly running on less than fumes?

"Was I supposed to come running to you, Tam? What would you have done had I told you your father just threatened to take not only my scholarships away, but Zach's and Kayla's as well?"

She leveled his gaze. "I don't know what I would've done, but I know I would've fought. I assumed that the love we shared wasn't one-sided."

Instead of grabbing hold of her and shaking her to make her listen like he wanted to, Cole placed his hands on his hips. "You know it wasn't one-sided. I've never loved anyone like you, Tam. You were it for me."

A laugh escaped her lips. The gesture didn't go with the emptiness in her baby blues.

"Was I? Should I consider myself lucky?" She threw her arms wide. "I feel sorry for all the other women you've had in your life if that's how you treat 'the one.'"

He deserved her wrath, he knew it, but he wouldn't stand in his own home and allow his past to be thrown back into his face.

"Your father made it impossible for me to choose," he argued. "My family had to come first. We didn't have everything handed to us."

Like you did.

He didn't have to say the words, they hovered in the air between them anyway. Yes, it was a low jab, but it was also the truth.

She sighed, stepped aside to focus once again on the stunning view. "I don't know why we're arguing. If it was meant to be, we'd have found our way back to each other. I'm just surprised that you let anyone get the best of you."

"I'm not that man anymore." He never would be. "And you're right. Arguing won't change the past and we're different people now."

Well, other than the fact that he still found her impossibly gorgeous and sexier than any woman should have the right to be.

Not to mention she'd burned him up in his bed, even though he was quick to douse any flame that could ignite into something more…at least in her mind. He didn't want to lead her on.

No matter what Tamera said, she was a "happily ever after" girl. Once her father passed, she would have nothing holding her back and she would need someone to lean on for support…even if she didn't want to admit it. Tamera was a strong woman, one of the strongest he knew, but even the sturdiest needed support during a storm.

She turned sideways, facing him once again. Shoulders back, chin tilted, she said, "Once this project is over, I never want to see you again. I won't be made a fool of twice. But we'll give Victor the best design he's ever had because we're both good at our jobs. Don't think for a second, though, that I trust you…with anything."

"I didn't ask for your trust, Tamera." He clenched his fist in his pocket as he searched her face for something…

anything, but all he saw was bitterness. "This project is all that matters."

She turned to walk out, but stopped just as her foot hit the bottom step of his living room. She threw a glance over her shoulder.

"You were wrong. You're still the same person. All that matters is money and yourself. I just didn't see that's who you were back then." She bit her lip, her chin quivered. "What a lonely world."

The echoing of her heels died with the final click of his front door. He would not feel guilty about the truth coming out. If anything, relief swept through him.

Once they delivered this design to Victor, and it was officially approved, then Zach would take over and Cole could officially close the book on his past and any present involvement with Tamera Stevens.

But would this ache in his chest linger long after that?

Seventeen

Binders upon binders of building materials cluttered Tamera's desk and her boardroom table. Nothing was just jumping out and screaming "multimillion-dollar fantasy resort."

An idea slammed into her. Tamera picked up her cell and dialed an old friend who would certainly be able to help in this respect.

"Hello."

"Kayla? This is Tamera. You know that lunch date we mentioned?"

Cole's sister laughed. "I certainly do. When do you want to meet?"

"How about now?" She glanced at the clock on her desk. "I can have something delivered."

"Now is perfect. I just got done meeting with Victor and my brain is fried. I'll grab something from the deli next to the office. What do you want?"

Tamera gave Kayla her order and hung up. Cole would be furious that he was not included in this little impromptu meeting, but she wasn't too concerned with what Cole thought of her right now. Kayla was the decorator and Kayla was the one she needed to consult with.

If Cole stepped through her door, Tamera feared she'd unleash her fury on him. She'd definitely gone easy on him considering he'd damaged her heart so long ago. She'd mended it just fine and didn't need a replay.

But what really irked her in ways she couldn't even express was the fact he'd gone and slept with her anyway. Twice. Even after betraying her, giving her up, he still thought he could have her when he wanted. And she'd fallen right for his seduction. She'd practically begged for him to seduce her.

Jerk. Yes, she should take a portion of the blame, but she wasn't. All of this mess was his doing.

Tamera stood up from her desk, dropped her cell back into her purse on the floor at her feet and moved around the room.

What she really needed was some female bonding time. It had been so long since she'd really talked to a woman, and her elderly assistant didn't count.

The topic of Cole couldn't come up. She couldn't talk to Kayla about her older brother. Not right now when her emotions were still so open and hurtful.

Did Kayla know about the reasoning behind Cole's breakup? Had everyone known but her? Not that it mattered at this point in time, but, well, it did.

Tamera walked from her desk to the table she'd made a mess of. She closed a few of the binders with samples and pictures of past projects and moved them onto one of the chairs. She could certainly rule out several samples that just wouldn't fit in the fantasy, sexy role this hotel would play.

A light tap on her office door had Tamera jerk her head. Kayla stood in the doorway holding a plastic bag.

"Lunch," she said with a wide smile holding the bag up. "Looks like I'm just in time to save you from yourself."

Tamera laughed. "And I just cleared a spot for our lunch."

Cole's sister was a knockout. She had that coal black hair and those chocolate brown eyes like her brothers. She also had that bronzed skin that had nothing to do with spending time on the beach and everything to do with an awesome gene pool.

"How was the meeting with Victor?" Tamera asked as Kayla pulled out the two chicken salads. "Are you eager to get started on your part with him?"

Kayla flopped into a vacant chair and sighed. "I'm not sure about that. He's a bit…intimidating."

Tamera took a seat, opened the salads and passed one across the table. "That's because you're so quiet. Don't be afraid of someone with all that power, Kayla. You underestimate your own strength."

Strength that was a family trait.

No, no. She wasn't going to think about Cole right now.

"I know I'm good at what I do," Kayla said, stabbing a cherry tomato. "I just don't know if I can handle the way he was looking at me."

Tamera froze, mid-bite. "Looking at you?"

Kayla closed her eyes. "I know it's my imagination."

"Why don't you tell me and I'll let you know if you're imagining things."

Kayla took a bite, chewed, and Tamera figured the woman was trying to figure out the best way to tell the story without sounding conceited.

"Forget it." Kayla jabbed her fork into her salad. "It's not even worth discussing. Tell me what's happening on your end. How is it working with my brother again?"

So much for not talking about Cole.

Tamera chose her words carefully. "It's been a good thing for this project."

Kayla gave her an "oh, really" look. "Now tell me the truth. What has this been like on a personal level?"

"Honestly? It has been trying at times. Your brother is so…so…"

"I know." Kayla smiled, reached over and patted Tamera's hand. "He's been that way since the two of you broke up. Nothing gets in his way, nothing is ever good enough and he doesn't settle for anything that isn't the absolute best."

Again, Tamera chose her words carefully. "Did he ever tell you why we broke up?"

She really hoped Kayla hadn't known. She didn't know why, but just the thought of everyone being in the know but her really bothered her.

Kayla shook her head as she chewed. "He just said that he realized you needed more than he could offer and we were never allowed to mention you or the breakup again. He wanted to move past it completely. I do believe Zach knows the real reason. Those two are like one being. I've never seen closer siblings."

The knife Cole had jammed into her heart years ago just turned again. She shouldn't have pain every time she thought of or spoke of the man.

Tamera pasted a smile on her face. "Well, it was a

long time ago. I'm sure he's fallen in love numerous times since."

Kayla continued to study her salad as she poked around. "Not really. Sometimes he'd bring a woman around, but nothing serious. He's too busy building our empire and moving on to the next big project."

Well, at least he'd had something to occupy his lonely nights. Bastard.

Not that she was going to remain bitter. Her feelings for Cole had died long ago when he'd turned his back on her with lame excuses. And now that she knew the truth, she wouldn't give him another thought…at least not on a personal level.

Her desk phone rang shrilly, cutting into her thoughts.

"Excuse me," she said, getting up from the table. She crossed to her desk, reached across and hit the speaker button. "Hello."

"I've got the afternoon free. Come down to my office so we can work on the materials."

Tamera threw a look to Kayla and rolled her eyes. "Gee, your manners have me ready to toss aside my current meeting to jump at the chance to get to your office."

Kayla laughed.

"Kayla?" Cole asked. "Is my sister there?"

Tamera smiled. "Yes."

"Why?"

All joking was gone from his tone. Tamera grabbed the receiver. No need to let Kayla know how much they weren't getting along.

"Because I needed another opinion," she told him, keeping her tone chipper.

"I'm your partner on this, Tamera. Calling one of my siblings was not professional or acceptable."

Tamera gripped the phone and turned her back on Kayla. "I'm doing what's best for this project. If you have a problem, then it's your problem. If there's nothing else you need, I have to get back to my meeting."

"I'm on my way."

He hung up and Tamera had to take deep, calming breaths in order to face Kayla again.

"Sorry he's so insufferable."

Kayla's tone was laced with worry, her brows drawn together.

Coming back to the table and the lunch she no longer cared about, Tamera shrugged and took her seat. "It's not your fault he's so overbearing. He's coming over, by the way."

"I could've told you he'd do that. He's also very competitive." Kayla gathered the garbage from their lunch, stuffing it into a sack. "He wants to be in on this project from the beginning to the end, no matter what his part is in this company."

"I can't imagine Zach will put up with Cole hanging around the job site," Tamera commented.

"Oh, he and Zach have had their fair share of arguments. Two Type A personalities like that? It can get pretty ugly. And they tend to save their aggressions for family meals and office meetings."

"How lovely for you."

Tamera laughed, earning a laugh from Kayla. Tamera marveled at how easy and fun it was falling back into a sisterly pattern with Kayla.

"I'm sorry we lost touch," Tamera said, dropping all joking from her tone. "That's my fault. After Cole and I broke up, I just couldn't…"

"I understand." Kayla leaned back in her chair. "It's none of my business what happened with you two, but I have to say, I feel like we broke up as well."

Guilt overwhelmed her. "I'm so sorry, Kayla. I thought about calling you, but I really didn't know what to say."

"It's okay, really. How's your father? Cole says he's sick."

Tamera nodded. "He's not well at all. He's in Mercy Hospice."

Kayla's head tilted. "That's what Cole told us. I can't imagine what all you're going through. Is there anything you need me to do?"

"No. Just being a friend is good enough."

"Is this a Dr. Phil show or a work place?"

Kayla and Tamera both turned their attention toward the door as Cole came gliding right in as if he owned the place.

"Looks like I arrived just in time. Have either of you done anything but reminisce?"

Kayla stood up, crossed to kiss her brother on his cheek. "Don't be such a grouch. Tamera and I haven't really spoken in a long time. We'll get to work."

"How did your meeting with Victor go?" he asked.

"Well," Kayla shrugged with a laugh. "He certainly knows what he wants."

Cole smiled down at his sister. Tamera wondered why he never smiled at her in that genuine, you-matter-to-me sort of way. Granted they had argued most of the time lately, but even when good things happened, he still hadn't looked at her like she meant something to him.

Guess those intimate moments in his bed hadn't even warranted a genuine grin every now and then. Work, work, work. And he thought *she* needed to lighten up?

"We really have to get cracking on this." Cole pulled out a seat, taking it only after his sister had sat back down. "I'm actually glad you're here, Kayla. Since you met with Victor, you have a better idea of what we're striving toward."

So, this was a good idea that Kayla was here? Of course, Cole wouldn't thank Tamera or tell her this was a good move. No, having Kayla here wasn't his idea, so thankfulness would be absent from this meeting.

That was just fine. She didn't need anything from Cole other than his mind for business.

She just hated that, deep down, she really couldn't get their past off her mind. She'd been so in love, she would've given up anything to be with him.

Why was she dwelling on this? Why didn't she just cut her losses and move on? Obviously Cole had.

But Kayla's words came back through her mind.

He's never fallen in love since you. He's had girls, but nothing serious.

In eleven years?

"You with us, Tam?"

She jerked herself from her thoughts and focused on Cole's questioning gaze. "Where else would I be?"

Eighteen

Victor Lawson's party was no less extravagant than his buildings. Tamera exited her chauffeur-driven limo, compliments of Mr. Lawson, and smiled to the young gentleman who'd taken her hand to assist her from the car.

Victor also lived on Star Island, big surprise. Well, lived was probably not the right choice of words. This was just one of his many luxury homes, Tamera was sure.

She'd received her invitation to Victor's party a week ago and didn't think twice about attending. The last time she'd been on Star Island she hadn't needed the invitation to get past the guard and onto the bridge. She'd only needed one man.

Tamera shook off thoughts of Cole and his betrayal. She couldn't think of that now. No way would she allow the hurt to creep up and consume her while she was here. This was too nice of an evening to let it get tainted by past memories.

Instead, she focused on the beauty of the home. Much like Cole's, Victor's house had that cozy, Mediterranean feel. Perhaps that was why he approved their initial design for the hotel so wholeheartedly.

Tamera made her way through the arched entryway from the circular drive and was greeted by none other than Victor himself.

"Stunning as always, Tamera."

Victor took both her hands in his, kissed her cheek and escorted her inside.

"This is a beautiful home, Victor. Thanks for the invitation."

She took in the high ceilings, the two sprawling staircases on either side of the formal entryway and the ginormous chandelier casting a kaleidoscope of colors onto the white marble flooring.

"There's no way I could throw a party and not invite my top architectural firms."

Just what she wanted. Another encounter with Cole.

"Kayla and her brother Zach just arrived. Cole has yet to show, but I'm sure he'll be along shortly."

He led her through the living area and out onto the patio where several people mingled with drinks and staff moved about with small, silver trays full of champagne. There was a spread of food on either side of the immaculate, glowing pool.

"I must tend to some other arrivals," Victor told her. "Please, eat, mingle. We'll talk later, but no shop talk tonight."

She smiled back at this handsome billionaire. "Sounds good."

As he walked away, Tamera wondered why her heart couldn't go pitty-pat at the sight of him instead of Cole. Why did the one man on this earth whose eyes she wanted to gouge out make her knees go weak, make her insides get all squishy like a teenage girl's on prom night?

"Tamera."

She turned at the sound of Zach's voice. "Evening, Zach. No lady attached to your arm this evening?"

Zach's laid-back appearance would only fly on him. No tie, white dress shirt unbuttoned two buttons beneath his black suit. This was as dressed up as Zach would get. Even though the man could afford tailor-made suits, he didn't want them. And she had no doubt he rode here on one of his Harleys.

"Actually, my date for tonight is my lovely sister."

Tamera laughed. "I'm impressed. And where is Kayla?"

"She went to talk to a potential client about redesigning their new home."

Tamera glanced around, finally spotting the exotic, gorgeous Kayla off in the distance talking with a middle-aged lady. As usual, Kayla was smiling and nodding, always eager to please clients.

"I'm not sure how much longer she'll be my date tonight if Victor keeps looking at her like he's been doing."

Tamera jerked back around. "Really? Isn't that interesting. She mentioned something like that to me the other day. Victor is used to beautiful women, and your sister is certainly no exception."

Zach took a long pull of his domestic beer. "I figured you and Cole would come together."

"Why would you assume that?" Tamera took a glass of champagne from one of the wait staff walking by.

"Because you've been awfully close lately."

"We're working on the biggest project either of our companies has ever seen. Besides, I doubt Cole and I will be seeing much of each other once the hotel is completed."

Zach took a long pull of his beer. "That's still a long way off. A lot could happen between now and then."

A lot *had* happened.

"Considering my part with Cole is drawing to a close, I don't foresee us working together in the future."

Zach leaned closer to whisper in her ear. "I don't know what Cole has told you, but trust me, he doesn't give up as easily as he used to."

What was that supposed to mean? Did she even want to know?

Cole's twin eased back, pointed with his longneck bottle toward the open patio doors. "Your partner has arrived."

By the time Tamera looked over her shoulder, cringed and turned back, Zach had walked away in the direction of a leggy blonde.

Tamera took a deep breath. If Cole wanted to approach her, fine. No way was she going to him.

Nursing her drink, Tamera walked around the pool, nodding and say hello to a couple of clients she'd worked with in the past. When she spotted Kayla moving away from her own potential client, Tamera made her way over.

"Well, did she like your ideas?" Tamera asked.

Kayla shrugged with a warm smile. "She seemed very interested in what I had to say, so I certainly hope so. Is this house amazing or what?"

Tamera laughed. "It is very nice."

"I thought Cole's was nice, but this is huge."

Even the mention of his name sent dual emotions racing through her. Anger and passion chased each other to be the one on top.

"Are you okay?" Kayla asked with that sweet, buttery tone she'd always had. "Cole told me about…well, what happened in the past. I honestly didn't know. He finally told me why the tension between the two of you is so much stronger now."

"I've been better," Tamera confessed. "It's hard to deal with something eleven years after the fact. I'm honestly not quite sure how to handle it or what I should be feeling."

Kayla put her arm around Tamera's shoulder and squeezed. "If it means anything, Cole has been in a really, really bad mood lately. That's good for you."

Tamera laughed. "How is that?"

"Because nothing ever bothers him." Kayla's eyes drifted off into the distance toward her brother. "You must matter even more than he cares to admit. Even to himself."

Squeezing the crystal stem of her glass, Tamera allowed her eyes to follow Kayla's. "Maybe so, but I don't like decisions being made for me that affect my entire life. Besides, he made his choice long ago when he didn't come back to me after school."

Kayla's arm dropped as she came to stand directly in front of Tamera. "Be that as it may, don't let the past direct your future."

Tamera looked into the dark eyes that were so much like Cole's. "I just can't concentrate on him and this whole mess. Not right now."

"I'm sorry about your father. Please let me know if there's anything I can do."

Tamera smiled at her longtime friend. "I appreciate that."

"Ladies."

Tamera cringed, then pasted on a smile as Cole came to stand beside them. "Cole."

"I think I landed another client," Kayla chimed in. "She's new to the Miami area, just bought a house in Coral Gables and is looking for a designer. My name was tossed her way."

"That's wonderful, Kayla," Cole said, kissing his sister on the cheek. "One of these days you'll be too big for me and Zach."

"Oh, I doubt that." Kayla's eyes darted from Tamera to Cole and back again. "I do think, though, that you two need to talk and I'm definitely the third wheel to this party."

Tamera's heart sank. The dead last thing she wanted was another confrontation with Cole about something that happened eleven years ago. And at Victor Lawson's home? That would be like career suicide because she knew once she and Cole started arguing again, they may never stop. God knew she had a great deal of anger and hatred right now and she was just waiting to unleash it.

"She never did like confrontation," Cole murmured as he watched his sister walk away.

Tamera narrowed her eyes when he directed his attention back to her. "I wasn't going to confront her with anything. She's never betrayed me."

Never one to back down, Cole held her gaze. "Neither have I."

"Really?" Tamera glanced around. Everyone was still

mingling, paying no attention to the feud in the corner. "And what do you call what you did?"

"Protecting my family."

Tamera sighed. "Forget it. I don't want an explanation. Not now. I'm too far gone to care."

"You care," he countered, leaning in so only she could hear. "You care too much and it's eating at you. You know I did what I had to do at the time. If you want to place blame somewhere, place it with your father."

"How are Miami's top architects doing?" Victor interrupted. "No shop talk, I hope?"

Cole eased back, smiled. "Not at all. Just discussing family. You have siblings, Victor?"

"A brother."

Cole nodded. "I was just telling Ms. Stevens how I'd do anything for my family. I'm sure you feel the same."

"Absolutely," Victor agreed. "My brother is all I have left and we are very close. What about you, Tamera, any family?"

Tamera swallowed. "Just my father."

"Daddy's girl, huh? He must be proud of you to follow in his footsteps and take over the family business. It's a shame I haven't gotten a chance to talk to him during this project. I thought for sure we'd meet up again."

Tamera ignored Cole's hard stare and concentrated on Victor. "Have you met my father?"

"Of course. When I first started making money, I had your father design a home for my parents. I wanted to give them a nice house after all they'd done for me. I was able to do so with the help of your father."

See? She wanted to shout to Cole. Walter Stevens was a good man.

"Now probably isn't the best time to share this news,"

Tamera started. "But, my father actually isn't doing very well at all, that's why you haven't seen him."

"Nothing too serious, I hope."

Tamera's eyes darted to Cole, then back to Victor. Her voice softened. "He's in hospice. I'm sorry I didn't tell you at the start of the project, but you were fine working with me and I hope this won't affect our working relationship."

Victor's eyes widened. "Absolutely not. I'm terribly sorry about Walter. He's a good man, a fighter. Please, give him my regards when you see him again."

Great, now tears were clogging the back of her throat. She took one last sip of champagne and offered a smile to the men.

"I really need to get going. Thanks for having me, Victor. Cole."

Before either man could say anything or, heaven forbid, try to stop her, she moved across the moss-and-stone-covered patio, through the doors and headed to the front of the house to the row of limousines. She needed to get out of here.

If it wasn't one emotion piling up on her, it was another. Her father, her past, her present. When would this nightmare come to an end?

God, was she really praying for an end? How selfish was that?

Tamera stepped back into the limo and tried to relax as the chauffeur took her home. But all she could see when she closed her eyes was Cole. Cole when he made love to her, Cole when he tried to comfort her, Cole when he defended himself to her because of his love for his family.

Why couldn't the man just have stayed in the past?

Nineteen

The shrill phone cut through the darkness, jerking Tamera awake.

This was it. The call she'd been dreading. She knew it before she reached across her bed to the nightstand.

"Hello."

"Tamera, this is Camille, the night nurse at Mercy."

Tamera fell back onto her plush pillow. Her hand shook as she clutched the phone. "He's gone."

She didn't ask—she didn't want to hear her worst fears confirmed.

"I'm sorry. We called the funeral home and they are on their way."

Tamera shoved aside the remorse and hurt. She'd have time to deal with her own feelings later. Right now she had to make sure her father was taken care of.

"I'll be there in just a minute."

Tamera disconnected the call and gathered courage to take the first step from her bed. Putting her body on autopilot was the only way she'd get through these next few hours, days. Years.

She pulled a red cotton sundress over her head and slipped into her brown, beaded flip-flops. No time for grooming or any other maintenance like hair, makeup. None of that truly mattered, not in the grand scheme of things. She wanted to get to the hospice center before they took her father's…body.

God, those words didn't sound right even running through her head. This didn't happen to her. Things like this happened to other people. Other people lost loved ones.

Now she was truly all alone. There was no one else in her family.

Tamera took a deep breath, grabbed her keys and purse and headed out to her garage. She couldn't think about what she was doing in the middle of the night while the rest of Miami slept…or partied. Life went on even though her father's had ended and her world would never be the same.

She'd never hear his voice, never have a proud career moment she could share with him and get his nod of approval. Gone. He was just gone.

Before she knew it, she was pulling into the parking lot. Another deep breath and she killed the engine and tugged on the door handle.

She could do this. She had to. There was no one else.

As soon as she hit the nurses' station, Camille came around the desk and put an arm around her.

"The folks from the funeral home haven't arrived, yet. I'm so sorry, Tamera."

Tamera swallowed the lump of hurt. And while she appreciated the nurse's comfort, Tamera knew if she broke down now, she may never stop. "I knew this moment was coming."

"But it doesn't make it any easier," the nurse said, guiding her down the stark white hallway.

"No, it doesn't."

Camille paused outside the closed door. "I'll let you go in and have a moment to yourself."

Tamera nodded her appreciation, unable to express her thanks aloud for fear of losing it right here in the hallway.

Once the nurse went back down the hall, Tamera opened the door. She didn't know what she expected, but seeing her father lying on his bed didn't bother her as much as she thought it would.

He looked as though he were sleeping. Peacefully.

On shaky legs, Tamera crossed the room and tugged the blanket up around his shoulders.

Peace. He'd finally found it. Something about that fact put Tamera at ease as well. Yes, her life wouldn't be the same without him, but it was selfish of her to want him back when he'd just been living in pain. He'd lived a happy, full life and done all the things he wanted to do.

She knelt over the bed, kissed his forehead. Her lips lingered, not wanting to break any bond.

"I love you, Daddy," she whispered. "I forgive you."

Cole hung up the phone. He'd been calling every day since he and Tamera had their blowup to check on Walter. He knew when the old man passed Tamera wouldn't confide in him, so he'd had to keep himself in the loop on his own.

But now Walter was gone and Cole couldn't bring himself to be remorseful.

But Tamera had to feel all alone…she was alone now with no family left. Who would she turn to? Who would offer her a shoulder to cry on, lean on?

Cole wished she'd come to him, but he wasn't naïve enough to believe she'd trust him with anything, especially her feelings, ever again.

And that was fine. Really. In the grand scheme of things, he didn't have time for a relationship, especially one with so much baggage. They'd have to work doubly hard and he really didn't have time or the patience for that type of commitment.

He would send flowers to the funeral home, and a personal bouquet and message to Tam's house. After that, their dealings would be in business only.

Though he did feel as if he should deliver her flowers in person. If nothing else, to make sure she was okay and to defend himself for the final time. Victor's party hadn't given him the right opportunity.

And there was one more thing. What he needed to do was catch her now, vulnerable and all, and make her see his side. Then perhaps he could persuade her to sell her father's company and work for him.

True, he didn't want the relationship consisting of anything that remotely resembled the "L" word, but she was one hell of a worker and Cole wanted her on his team. So long as the rest of The Stevens Group went by the wayside.

Cole pushed up from his sofa and went to dress. Tamera's father had passed away in the middle of the night, and seeing as how it was now ten in the morning, Tamera should be back home.

He quickly dressed, all the while running through his mind all he would and should say to her to sway her to see his point of view in the dealings so long ago and to get her to come over to his side.

In the mood for something a little less "businesslike," Cole grabbed the keys to his Jeep Wrangler. From his house on Star Island, it didn't take long to drive to Tamera's beachfront condo in South Beach, especially early on a Sunday morning.

He pulled in behind her car along the street and got out. He prepared himself for whatever state she may be in. Angry, depressed, shocked, numb. He was ready to console her no matter the emotions she was dealing with.

Cole rang the doorbell and waited. But when the door opened, he realized there was one emotion he'd overlooked. Emptiness.

He didn't wait for an invitation…not that he expected one. He walked through the door and put his arms around her.

"No." Tamera pulled back and turned away. "I don't want you to console me."

Cole stood rooted in place. Tam's rigid back and the steel in her tone concerned him.

"Don't be afraid to break, Tam." He stepped closer. "Crying and getting angry are perfectly normal emotions."

She spun around, her eyes red and swollen, but dry. "How did you know?"

"Does it matter?"

"I don't want you here."

"I'm sure you don't," he agreed. "But who else would you call to come be with you?"

Her chin tilted. "Who said I was going to call anyone? I'm just fine, Cole."

So be it.

"Good." He crossed his arms because he wanted to pull her against him and assure her everything would be fine. Stupid on his part. He didn't need to get tangled up anymore in this woman. "I assume the funeral will be this week."

She nodded, but her eyes remained fixed over his shoulder. She wasn't listening, wasn't comprehending what he was saying. She was running on little more than fumes and it wouldn't take long for her to collapse on this wall she'd built out of sand.

"If you need anything at all, call me. Don't shut me out because of your pride."

"I'm shutting you out because of *your* pride," she amended in a low, sad tone.

"I've put my pride aside. Can you say the same?"

"Put your pride aside?" She stood stone still. "You think by barging in here, hoping to catch me in an emotional meltdown, I'll collapse into your arms and we'll get past this?"

He told himself not to let her stinging words hurt or deter him. She was aching, grieving. Not thinking straight.

Or maybe her true feelings were just now coming out.

"Honestly," he began in a low voice. "I did want you to admit that you needed someone. And, yes, I wanted that someone to be me. I'm not asking you to deal with your father's death and our past all at once. I'm not a jerk, Tam, but I'm also not going to beg."

Once again, she stared and said nothing as he showed himself out. He'd let her think about that for a while. Pride and lies had gotten them in trouble before, he didn't make the same mistakes twice.

If she wanted to keep everything from here on out businesslike, then he would go along with her wishes. But he wouldn't make the process easy for her. Because he was finally coming to realize that maybe, just maybe, they did need each other in more than just the boardroom.

Rain poured down and Tamera willed her wipers to go faster. She had no clue where she was driving this morning, but she knew she couldn't go home. Not right now. She couldn't go into work, either. Not when her father's memories still lingered and hovered in every corner on every floor.

As her car passed over the bridge to Star Island, she realized what she was doing. She needed to do this. Now that her father's funeral had passed, Tamera knew life was too short to hold grudges. She'd forgiven her father, now she needed to forgive Cole.

With yesterday evening's funeral replaying over and over in her mind, Tamera knew today had to be a new beginning.

She pulled around the fountain in Cole's circular drive and killed her engine. Leaving her keys and her purse in her car, she hopped out. No need to take her things with her. What she came to say would only take a minute.

When she stepped from the car, rain pelted her skin, drenching her instantly. Her hair clung to her neck and shoulders.

But she just stood there. Everything about her life

played through her head. Her father holding her hand when her mother had passed away, her father teaching her to drive and dance. The moments when he'd taken time to show her his little secrets about the company she'd now inherited. The moment when the pallbearers settled her father's casket onto the platform at the cemetery.

The flowers and card from The Marcum Agency. Cole.

"Tamera."

Tamera turned her head toward Cole's voice. He stood in his doorway wearing nothing but a pair of running shorts.

And in the second he saw her face, he must've known. Even though they'd severed their connection from years ago, he still knew her heart and her vulnerabilities. He came out into the rain and pulled her into his embrace.

That was all it took. She wrapped her arms around his bare waist and clung to him, wishing she could draw strength from him. But all that happened was the meltdown that had been a long time coming.

No matter what had happened with Cole, she still had feelings for him. He was the only man she'd ever loved and she needed him right now. She needed that shoulder to cry on and she didn't care if he thought her weak. At this moment, she was.

"I'm sorry."

She'd been hearing those simple words so much over the past few days, but for some reason, coming from Cole's mouth, she believed him.

He kissed the top of her head and eased her back to study her drenched face. "Come in out of the rain."

Her eyes darted to his moist lips as the rain continued

to beat down on them. Desire like she'd never known coursed through her, fighting against the hurt and emptiness she'd been feeling for far too long.

Maybe she needed him more than she thought. She eased up on her toes to angle her mouth toward his.

"No," he said over the downpour. "That is not what you need."

"That's exactly what I need, Cole."

She framed his face with her hands and drew his lips down to hers. He didn't resist.

Cole's arms came around her, lifting her up off the driveway and flush against his taut, wet body. Her moment of control over this situation, if she ever really had it, was long gone and in Cole's hands. Which was fine with her.

She didn't want to think, didn't want to worry about anything but taking the comfort Cole had to offer. Didn't want to think about the actions and the events that led her straight to his door. Nor did she want to consider the reality that she was weak, vulnerable and Cole was the only rock in this storm she could cling to.

When he turned to carry her into the house, Tamera wrapped her legs around his waist, her arms around his neck. Toying with the wet hair at the nape of his neck, she kissed along his strong jaw. God, she'd missed him.

With a swift kick, he had the door closed and her pinned against it. But he kept his touch soft, light, as if he were afraid of breaking her. She couldn't break anymore than she already had.

"Don't be gentle with me," she demanded against his lips.

"I'm giving what you need." His husky tone and

warm breath excited her even more. "Whether you know it or not."

"I need you. Only you."

He peeled the wet straps down her arms, she tugged free of them as he pulled the garment below her breasts. She arched her back as he slid a hand behind her to unfasten her strapless bra and toss it without a care to the tile floor.

Reaching beneath the short hem of her sundress, he pulled at her bikini panties until they slid silently to the floor, leaving her bare for him.

His mouth ran from her neck down to the slope of her breasts. Tamera clutched his wet, messy hair with her fingers.

"Wait," she panted. "Condom."

"Relax. I've got you protected. Always."

The meaning behind his words was so much more than here and now, but she couldn't think about it, didn't want to get false hope.

Cole pulled her away from the door, took her hand and guided her up the wide, sweeping staircase. But Tamera didn't want to follow. She bypassed him in a mad dash toward his bedroom.

As soon as she crossed the threshold, she shimmied out of the dress, allowing it to fall to the tiled floor of his master suite with a wet slap. Cole's eyes raked over her bare body, the muscle in his jaw clenching as he crossed to the bedside table and pulled out a condom.

Tamera walked up behind him, kissed her way across his taut shoulders before falling back onto the bed in a provocative position. She raised slightly up onto her elbows, quirking a brow at him.

Cole tossed the condom onto her stomach. "Cover me."

Once he was ready, she guided him into her.

How could she ever think the two of them was a mistake? How had she not seen that she cared about this man more than she wanted to admit?

Cole captured her mouth once again as her body started rising toward its peak. She wrapped her legs around him once again and climaxed just before him.

Their bodies shuddered together as Cole placed a tender kiss to her lips. He lay on her body, chest to chest afterward, his fast, heavy breathing tickling the side of her neck.

"I didn't know where else to go," she murmured, afraid of the words and what they meant.

"I'm glad you came here." He lifted up, rolled to the side and rested his head on his hand. "I'm also sorry you're hurting."

Tamera didn't want to diminish the afterglow of their lovemaking, but she had to face reality. She had to tell him what was in her heart, and hopefully salvage the best part of the relationship they'd had and rebuild a life from there.

"I actually came to just tell you that I forgive you."

His eyes widened. "Really?"

She turned to her side to face him. "I can't live holding grudges and with Dad's passing, I know that life is too short to stay mad. Besides, being on friendly terms with you has its benefits."

His eyes roamed down the dip in her waist and over the swell of her hip. "Yes, it does."

He pushed her onto her back once again and showed her just how beneficial their friendship could be.

"I don't think I can handle this."

Tamera hadn't wanted to admit that to herself, much less aloud. But her fears were out in the open, in Cole's darkened bedroom. His roman shades had dropped at the click of a switch just after they'd made love in the glow of the sunset. But resting was something Tamera knew wouldn't happen for a long, long time.

Cole rolled from his back to his side. "This as in us?"

Tamera kept her eyes averted to the ceiling. She didn't want to face him, not when she was voicing her waking nightmare.

"Running the company without the guidance of my father."

Cole's gentle fingers cupped her chin and turned her head, forcing her to look him in the eye. "Then sell it."

"What?"

"Don't stress yourself," he told her. "If you feel like this is something that isn't right for you, then get out."

"But I love what I do."

Sell her father's legacy? Something he'd worked so hard for? How heartless would that be to consider selling his empire not a full week after his funeral?

"I know you love it," Cole told her, a hint of a smile playing around his mouth. "Come work for me."

Tamera jerked up in bed, the sheet falling to pool at her waist. "Work for you? I can't do that."

Cole sat up beside her. "Why not? We make a great team."

She'd already shown him her vulnerable side. Might as well lay it all on the line.

"Working for you isn't such a great idea, Cole." She gathered her courage from deep within as she clutched the sheet to her breasts. "Let's say I do sell my father's company and come to work for The Marcum Agency.

What happens if we don't get along? You know how we butt heads."

"We'll be fine. I argue all the time with Zach and Kayla. It's just part of powerful people working together, but the outcome is amazing when our clients' praise is heard worldwide."

He didn't get it.

"Let me put it this way," she said, holding his gaze. "What happens when you decide you don't want to be with me anymore?"

"Who says that will happen?"

She lifted a shoulder. "Happened before."

Cole closed the gap between them. "Not by my choice."

Tamera closed her eyes, not wanting to pull her father into this.

"I'm not going to discuss blame," he said as if he could read her mind. "But the reason I didn't tell you all those years ago was because I didn't want to come between you and your father and I knew his actions would drive a wedge between you."

She opened her eyes. "I didn't want to lose you, either, Cole. Didn't you know I would've done anything to be with you? That's what hurts the most is that you didn't believe in what we had enough to come to me. Obviously our relationship wasn't built on the trust and honesty I'd depended on."

"Maybe it wasn't," he agreed. "I know I loved you then, but that point in time doesn't even compare to what I'm feeling now."

Tamera turned away, scared to look into his eyes and see what she'd longed to see from him for so long. Love, commitment.

"I just don't know if my heart can take that chance

again, Cole," she whispered, wrapping her arms around her waist. "I want to. More than anything I want to be what you need, because you're certainly what I need. But not at the risk of being broken again."

Cole's hand covered her shoulder. He turned her to face him, and she found herself looking up into his dark eyes. Eyes that held so much hope, the same hope that she knew was reflected in her own stare.

"I was a fool." He ran a fingertip down her cheek. "I won't be a fool twice, Tamera. I love you. Marry me. Let me have a lifetime to make it up to you. Let me show you how special you are to me, how much I need you in my life. I can't function without you. I've tried. The monotony from day to day was meaningless. I need you to fill that void that was left so long ago. Say you'll marry me."

She'd heard those words from his mouth before, but now, the proposal meant so much more. Now they mended every crack, every wound of her broken heart.

"You'll always be honest with me?" she asked.

"Always."

Tamera wrapped her arms around Cole's neck. "Yes, I'll marry you."

"Victor was right," he whispered in her ear.

"About?"

He urged her back into bed. "We make a great team."

Epilogue

"When you do something, you don't do halfway," Zach said, pulling a beer from Cole's office refrigerator.

Kayla poured champagne, passed out the glasses to Cole and Tamera. "They always worked well together. Now it's just carried on into their business."

"Speaking of that, what are you going to do, Tamera?"

Tamera looked to Cole's twin and smiled. "You haven't mentioned this?"

Cole nuzzled her neck. "I've been preoccupied completing a design and keeping a certain woman happy."

"Someone better tell us something," Zach piped in. "Kayla and I are getting uncomfortable in here."

Cole straightened, addressing his siblings. "We'd like to merge the firms together since we're merging the families."

Tamera held her breath, awaiting the reaction of two-thirds of The Marcum Agency's approval.

"We'd definitely monopolize the architectural world of Miami," Zach stated, rubbing a hand over his stubbled jaw. "I think it's a great business move. Kayla?"

Kayla beamed. "I vote yes."

Cole grinned, winking at Tamera. "Told you it wouldn't be a problem. We're still simple people who know when we see a good thing."

Zach raised his beer. "To mergers."

Champagne flutes clinked together in the air. "To mergers," they all agreed.

"May the next part of this project be as exciting as the design."

Tamera laughed. "Zach, you'll make the next stage exciting no matter what the circumstances are."

"Don't make it too exciting," Cole countered. "We don't want our wedding in a few months overshadowed by anything."

"Trouble," Zach said, "is like women. It just follows me."

Cole simply shook his head, laughed and kissed Tamera. "He's on his own. I have more important things to attend to."

* * * * *

COMING NEXT MONTH

Available November 9, 2010

#2047 THE MAVERICK PRINCE
Catherine Mann
Man of the Month

#2048 WEDDING HIS TAKEOVER TARGET
Emilie Rose
Dynasties: The Jarrods

#2049 TEXAS TYCOON'S CHRISTMAS FIANCÉE
Sara Orwig
Stetsons & CEOs

#2050 TO TAME A SHEIKH
Olivia Gates
Pride of Zohayd

#2051 THE BILLIONAIRE'S BRIDAL BID
Emily McKay

#2052 HIGH-SOCIETY SEDUCTION
Maxine Sullivan

REQUEST YOUR FREE BOOKS!

2 FREE NOVELS
PLUS 2
FREE GIFTS!

Passionate, Powerful, Provocative!

YES! Please send me 2 FREE Silhouette Desire® novels and my 2 FREE gifts (gifts are worth about $10). After receiving them, if I don't wish to receive any more books, I can return the shipping statement marked "cancel." If I don't cancel, I will receive 6 brand-new novels every month and be billed just $4.05 per book in the U.S. or $4.74 per book in Canada. That's a saving of at least 15% off the cover price! It's quite a bargain! Shipping and handling is just 50¢ per book.* I understand that accepting the 2 free books and gifts places me under no obligation to buy anything. I can always return a shipment and cancel at any time. Even if I never buy another book, the two free books and gifts are mine to keep forever.

225/326 SDN E5QG

Name	(PLEASE PRINT)	
Address		Apt. #
City	State/Prov.	Zip/Postal Code

Signature (if under 18, a parent or guardian must sign)

Mail to the **Silhouette Reader Service:**
IN U.S.A.: P.O. Box 1867, Buffalo, NY 14240-1867
IN CANADA: P.O. Box 609, Fort Erie, Ontario L2A 5X3

Not valid for current subscribers to Silhouette Desire books.

Want to try two free books from another line?
Call 1-800-873-8635 or visit www.morefreebooks.com.

* Terms and prices subject to change without notice. Prices do not include applicable taxes. N.Y. residents add applicable sales tax. Canadian residents will be charged applicable provincial taxes and GST. Offer not valid in Quebec. This offer is limited to one order per household. All orders subject to approval. Credit or debit balances in a customer's account(s) may be offset by any other outstanding balance owed by or to the customer. Please allow 4 to 6 weeks for delivery. Offer available while quantities last.

Your Privacy: Silhouette Books is committed to protecting your privacy. Our Privacy Policy is available online at www.eHarlequin.com or upon request from the Reader Service. From time to time we make our lists of customers available to reputable third parties who may have a product or service of interest to you. If you would prefer we not share your name and address, please check here. ☐

Help us get it right—We strive for accurate, respectful and relevant communications. To clarify or modify your communication preferences, visit us at www.ReaderService.com/consumerschoice.

SDES10R

HARLEQUIN®

A Romance

FOR EVERY MOOD™

Spotlight on

Inspirational

Wholesome romances
that touch the heart and soul.

See the next page
to enjoy a sneak peek from
the Love Inspired® Suspense
inspirational series.

*See below for a sneak peek from
our inspirational line, Love Inspired® Suspense*

*Enjoy this heart-stopping excerpt from
RUNNING BLIND
by top author Shirlee McCoy,
available November 2010!*

**The mission trip to Mexico was supposed to be an
adventure. But the thrill turns sour when Jenna Dougherty
and her roommate Magdalena are kidnapped.**

"It's okay. I'm here to help." The voice was as deep as the
darkness, but Jenna Dougherty didn't believe the lie. She
could do nothing but lie still as hands slid down her arms,
felt the rope around her wrists.

"I'm going to use a knife to cut you free, Jenna. Hold
still."

The cold blade of a knife pressed close to her head before
her gag fell away.

"I—" she started, but her mouth was dry, and she could
do nothing but suck in air.

"Shhh. Whatever needs to be said can be said when
we're out of here." Nick spoke quietly, his hand gentle on
her cheek. There and gone as he sliced through the ropes on
her wrists and ankles.

He pulled her upright. "Come on. We may be on
borrowed time."

"I can't leave my friend," Jenna rasped out.

"There's no one here. Just us."

"She has to be here." Jenna took a step away.

"There's no one here. Let's go before that changes."

"It's dark. Maybe if we find a light…"

"What did you say?"

"We need to turn on the light. I can't leave until I know that—"

"What can you see, Jenna?"

"Nothing."

"No shadows? No light?"

"No."

"It's broad daylight. There's light spilling in from the window I climbed in through. You can't see it?"

She went cold at his words.

"I can't see anything."

"You've got a nasty bruise on your forehead. Maybe that has something to do with it." His fingers traced the tender flesh on her forehead.

"It doesn't matter *how* it happened. I'm blind!"

Can Nick help Jenna find her friend or will chasing this trail have Jenna running blindly again into danger?

Find out in RUNNING BLIND, available in November 2010 only from Love Inspired Suspense.

FROM #1 *NEW YORK TIMES*
AND *USA TODAY* BESTSELLING AUTHOR

DEBBIE MACOMBER

Mrs. Miracle on 34th Street…

This Christmas, Emily Merkle (just call her Mrs. Miracle) is working in the toy department at Finley's, the last family-owned department store in Manhattan.

Her boss (who happens to be the owner's son) has placed an order for a large number of high-priced robots, which he hopes will give the business a much-needed boost. In fact, Jake Finley's counting on it.

Holly Larson is counting on that robot, too. She's been looking after her eight-year-old nephew, Gabe, ever since her widowed brother was deployed overseas. Holly plans to buy Gabe a robot—which she can't afford—because she's determined to make Christmas special.

But this Christmas will be different—thanks to Mrs. Miracle. Next to bringing children joy, her favorite activity is giving romance a nudge. Fortunately, Jake and Holly are receptive to her "hints." And thanks to Mrs. Miracle, Christmas takes on new meaning for Jake. For all of them!

Call Me Mrs. Miracle

Available wherever books are sold
September 28!

MIRA®